A HAUNT OF JACKALS

D0950397

A HAUNT OF JACKALS

Paul deParrie

CROSSWAY BOOKS•WHEATON, ILLINOIS
A DIVISION OF GOOD NEWS PUBLISHERS

Acknowledgments

I would like to thank Jan Dennis from Crossway Books, Barbara Thompson, and Mettie Williams for their invaluable assistance and critique. Lila Bishop's incisive editing helped bring warmth to the characters and more cogency to the story. Without their help, I would not have been able to enter this vastly different world of fiction writing.

A Haunt of Jackals

Copyright © 1991 by Paul deParrie

Published by Crossway Books, a division of
Good News Publishers, Wheaton, Illinois 60187.

Cover illustration: David Yorke

First printing, 1991

Printed in the United States of America

Library of Congress Cataloging-in-Publication Data
deParrie, Paul.
   A haunt of jackals / Paul deParrie.
      p.   cm.
    I. Title.
PS3554.E5927H3 1991 813'.54—dc20   90-20944
ISBN 0-89107-605-0

99		98		97		96		95		94		93		92		91
15	14	13	12	11	10	9	8	7	6	5	4	3	2	1

To
Andrew Burnett
and
Dawn Stover

JEREMIAH 9:7, 11A

Therefore this is what the Lord Almighty says:

"See, I will refine and test them,
for what else can I do because of the sin of my people?
. . . I will make [their land] a heap of ruins,

a haunt of jackals."

1 THE CONFLICT BEGINS

A spark!

Not as an electrical spark with its sudden blinding light, its equally sudden disappearance leaving only faint images shimmering on the retina.

Yet it was very like an electrical spark in its energy . . . only this energy continued, emitting Life rather than light. The two minuscule pieces, two living parts incapable of life alone, came together. And just as the two lovers who brought them together struggled in the darkness, so these two made the spark in the obscurity of the warm, dark passage.

Thus began the journey.

It was a blind groping; it appeared, though no eyes watched, to tumble aimlessly.

Since the first spark, there had been a chromosomal pattern that said Unique Human Being. This was no mere mirror of the two parts supplied by the lovers, but one unique blend, sharing something of each. The double X of the first cell "said" woman, and every other cell afterward echoed the refrain.

For days she busied herself copying the spark born of the two parts now one; doubling, doubling, doubling. She moved forward. She must hurry . . . or die. She tumbled—rolling—swimming—gleeful in the joy of being alive.

The DNA was a general, drumming out orders to the now thousands of sparks that, though all had differing functions, worked in concert. The thought behind the general's commands became evident.

We would not recognize it as thought, just as we do not recognize the thought behind our own bodies' commands to replenish, to reproduce skin cells, blood cells. We do not call it thought, though it is thought, that directs the heart to beat and the alveoli to draw oxygen from the lungs, delivering it to the bloodstream.

Until now all the thoughts had been self-directives: "Make a new cell," "All cells divide," and finally, "Cells, group into different kinds!"

Meanwhile the irresistible homing instinct drove her onward relentlessly until she arrived and firmly implanted herself in what her entire being called "home." No, it was more! It was "Home" with a capital "H," the safest place in the universe. Immediately upon arrival, she threw the switch for the menstrual cycle to "off," and she was safe!

Her mother was Clarissa Strauss.

*

Clarissa Strauss had been a mother for about seven hours. She did not know it. She donned her black and electric blue running outfit and stretched, preparing for her morning run. The door on their modest suburban home slammed behind her as she headed out for her jog in the bleak morning light. The breeze from the coast carried a faint salty aroma. Clarissa noted this with exhilaration, set her mind on autopilot, and cruised down the curved lane.

She was busily engaged in a thousand tiny things and

several large things, as with all who experience the ultimate mystery called Life. With Clarissa, as with most of us, it rarely appeared to be a mystery at all . . . because of the thousand little things and the several large ones. But she was nineteen and a half years old, newly married (six months, one week, and three days!), and she was just launching herself into a career in fashion clothing. *Sure, I'm only in sales here at Mayline . . . for now!* she punctuated the thought, *but this job has real possibilities.*

Clarissa remembered several go-nowhere jobs. They had been steps to attain her short-term, high-school-kid goals. On her first job she and her coworkers had laughed about "working under the fallen arches," long shifts of standing on the hard, tile floors while preparing hamburgers. She had to admit, her feet felt pretty much the same after a day selling frocks in the air-conditioned, plush-carpeted comfort of Mayline, the cutting-edge fashion outlet.

Later, after her run, Clarissa saw the same neighborhood streets again as she began her drive to work. The area had been a field with cows when she was very small, but she remembered the choking dust stirred by enormous machines as they groomed the area for houses. She had been in sixth grade at the time and would never have expected to be living in one of those very houses. *This used to be the edge of town,* she thought as she guided her car onto the main thoroughfare.

After arriving at work, Clarissa brushed her shoulder-length chestnut hair and did a last minute check of her appearance. Her own wide-set, hazel eyes looked back at her from the mirror in the corner of the crowded stock room. Her straight nose had been her bane in her early teens. A pert nose was considered the height of adolescent fashion. But as her features matured during her late teens,

Clarissa's face attained a rather sophisticated, almost European dimension that many described as "striking." She had always maintained a slim figure on her five-foot, seven-inch frame, but working with Mayline required more. They actually dictated the size each saleswoman should be; this was to "create the proper vision of the Mayline woman," said the instructor at the job orientation. Clarissa was at least two inches shorter than the standard "Mayline woman." The company felt that taller women exuded more authority about the fashions they were selling.

Certain qualities had enabled her to become the exception on the Mayline sales team. The effort she was putting in at night courses in the community college would pay off in a few years. She had a relaxed smile and sparkling wit combined with impeccable taste and a sense of fashion. She'd begun in the down-scale shop where she had worked, first part-time, then full-time, for the last two years. The Mayline job had opened shortly before her wedding.

In the I-am-immortal tradition of the young, Clarissa could see clearly the carefully mapped route of her future. Her husband, Matthew, and she had worked out their plans to a perfect dovetail. Matthew had not originally planned marriage for another year; however, after careful consideration he had seen that it could fit into his plans. So Clarissa felt secure. The tumultuous teens were over, and with them the lifelong uncertainty of her father's on-again, off-again construction work.

But she had her own sights set on becoming a buyer for Mayline. Despite her quick eye for the next trend and what was "right," her talents did not include a knack for actual design, so the practical side of Clarissa channeled her drive toward seeking out clothes for the market. It was an exciting and glamorous field, including globe-hopping and sampling the wares of the top designers—the *avant-garde*. She relished the thought of the places she would go—the people she would meet.

*

A short while ago she had been a sphere of cells, but then the outside cells drove inward and formed a neural tube. A spinal column now formed there. There was a bulb on the end of the column—the early form of the brain. Arm and leg buds protruded from the translucent body with its primal head. Dark eye cells congregated there. Her once tenuous hold on the uterine wall was now firmed by the near merging of the new placental cells weaving themselves into the living warp and woof of the uterus.

Her father's name was Matthew Strauss.

*

Matthew, two years Clarissa's senior, was moving up arduously in his father's company, but the climb was not easier for that fact. On the contrary, Father was more demanding of him than anyone else. It irked Clarissa whenever a less worthy person was promoted ahead of Matthew. He just chalked it up to good business practices.

Of course, they planned a family too. One, perhaps at most, two children, but that was over five years ahead in the schedule. Matthew and she had decided. They had concluded that they would not try to divide their attention among a whole bunch of screaming kids. "People need to aim for quality care for fewer children," they had agreed.

Matthew Strauss was like that, direct and purposeful, Clarissa knew. He seemed to have been born with goals and an unswerving energy directed toward them. To him, *purpose* was important. As a child he had not allowed himself to be called "Matt." Friends of his parents were amazed to hear the two-year-old insist, "I'm *Matthew*." When he was older, he explained that if his parents had intended to name him Matt, they would have done so. His true name was more dignified.

If anything characterized Matthew, it was his insistence on order. His squarish, blocky body along with the unruly straw hair and open, "farm-boy" face conspired to disguise this sense of dignity. However, it was this very sense of propriety that had left a blemish on his otherwise spotless school record.

Matthew had told Clarissa the story of how he had watched for days as his second grade teacher, Miss Danemore, futilely struggled to get Jimmy Davis to stop "cutting up" and show proper respect during flag salute (and practically everything else). Jimmy stood right behind Matthew on this fall morning whispering a silly poem during the salute. After first sh-sh-shing him, then muttering, "Shut UP," Matthew turned around between "under God" and "indivisible" and popped the offending mouth. It was poetic justice!

The rest of the world had ceased to exist for that moment as he stood in fighting stance over the felled form of his vanquished foe. When reality rushed back to his consciousness, he heard the o-o-oing and ah-h-ing of about twenty-five eight-year-olds and the laughter and snickering of six or seven others. It wasn't long before they were both snappily marched off, he to the principal's office, the lair of the notorious "Hatchet" Hackett, and the Davis boy limping off to see the nurse. Actually, Matthew's injuries probably far exceeded Jimmy's. Being untrained in the manly arts of warfare, Matthew had

curled his thumb inside his fist and wrenched the liga-
ments when he struck. Jimmy's hacksaw teeth had ripped
a gash across his knuckles, and he was bleeding (he
thought) profusely. Meanwhile, Jimmy, whose lip had
barely shed a couple of drops of blood, was under the tender care of Nurse Ellen.

So there Matthew sat, a huge puddle of blood growing beneath the big-person chair where he sat awaiting
sentencing in the antechamber of the dreaded principal's
office. But even then he felt justified, a feeling which (to
him) was confirmed later as Jimmy never again interrupted a flag salute, though he was still a "royal pain" to
Miss Danemore.

Matthew received "a good talking to" from Mr.
Hackett. As he left the office, Matthew knew that at this
very moment the electrical mysteries of the telephone
were carrying the famous "Hackett Hack," so often heard
crackling over the school public address system, to his
home and the astonished ears of his mother.

In the school the word was out; Matthew had "really
pounded" Jimmy Davis. Within a week Jimmy and
Matthew were best friends, a friendship that lasted
through their school years.

When Clarissa had heard the story, she said it was
cute. Matthew, on the other hand, did not regard it as
amusing but as a parable of life. Sometimes people suffer
for doing what's right.

Right now Matthew was pinching his neck trying to
button the top of his shirt before knotting his tie. "Ow!"
he exclaimed and finally brought the errant button home.
He heard the front door slam as Clarissa exited for her run.

Matthew now had been a father for about seven
hours. He did not know it.

*

She was "Home," but she did not rest. She had first commanded her mother's body to stop producing the prostaglandins that would start the menstrual period, but there were a thousand little things and several large things to do as well. She had to start her mother's system producing the many hormones to prepare her physically and, in subtle ways, mentally for motherhood. In order to be ready to nurse her child, the mother's body must begin preparations immediately. Baby gave the chemical command.

Three weeks from the first spark, she was already swimming in amniotic fluid attached by the tiny umbilical lifeline to her private food supply, the placenta. She could not hear her mother wondering why her period was late; she was too busy adding all the specialized cells for internal organs, eyes, and brain. There was also the continual stream of commands she sent to Mom.

*

Clarissa could not hear her daughter's commands, but her body slavishly obeyed them. "I've been a week late occasionally before," she frowned, hanging the expensive navy frock back on the rack, "but this is two weeks." Secretly she hoped that the deviation could be pinned on her new, more vigorous exercise regimen; she'd heard that often strenuous exercise slowed the menstrual cycle, causing late periods and, in extreme cases, stopped them altogether. But her career demanded that she keep that dress size down.

Clarissa thought back carefully and checked her pill dispenser during a slow moment at the store. *No, I haven't missed any,* she thought, knowing how methodical she had been. Birth control had not come naturally to Clarissa; it was a hard-won lesson.

Clarissa could still remember the tall, open, and amazingly fashionable middle-aged woman with her hair bobbed and just the right tint of silver. The woman had become an integral part of the "health" courses at Morrow High where Clarissa had attended. She had come often from the Family Life Association office scant blocks from Morrow, and as far as Clarissa knew, the woman still made her regular forays. She had been so self-assured saying, "There is only a 2 percent failure rate recorded for 'the pill,' and probably most of those failures can be traced to women who fail to follow instructions."

But Clarissa had paid little attention to the woman's exhortations; she intended to wait for marriage. The circumstances of the heart, however, were less than predictable. At sixteen, she fell in love with the junior varsity halfback. Giddily she wavered under the influence of the thought: *He's the only man for me.* Four or five torrid afternoons passed at her home—after school but before the folks returned from work. The following few weeks were the most anxious of her young life. She was fretting into the night, skittish by day. Mom and Dad were beginning to wonder.

Her period started. Safe!

"Never again!" she promised herself and then refused all offers, at least until she was sure of Matthew's intentions. She began taking the pill after a refresher course from Family Life about six months before her marriage.

But she remembered girls at Morrow who had suffered what they liked to call "pill failure"—though there had always been an unspoken assumption that it was, in fact, "girl failure." Some of these girls conveniently disappeared to "visit relatives" for a year. Others went to the Greenbriar Surgicenter operated by Dr. Jarvis, braving the frequent pickets to obtain a safe, legal abortion. A few girls boldly tossed their experience around as though it was a picnic or some bizarre rite of passage. Most fell curiously silent and found urgent things to do elsewhere when the topic arose.

Mary Willis had been like that—mute and withdrawing. She had been a close friend of Clarissa's since seventh grade when she first moved to town. As Clarissa began to arrange a new shipment on the racks, her mind drifted back to the day she had met Mary. It was the first day of school, with typical frantic confusion at the beginning of the year, plus for Mary a new school. As Mary entered the massive front doors, she looked for refuge. Across the scurrying, shoving, squashing sea of newly adolescent bodies, punctuated by the occasional spar of an adult frame, she spied an inviting door marked "Girls." Mary edged along the wall and, seeing the brief clearing, dashed across the hall. In her drive toward the double swinging doors, she neglected to heed the "in" and "out" signs. As she approached expecting to push, the door suddenly opened toward her, and she found herself sprawled on the floor amidst the flurry of her notebook paper fluttering to the floor.

Through Clarissa's profuse apologies and Mary's ritual "It's-all-right's," it occurred simultaneously to them how like a cartoon this episode must have looked to the others swarming the hall. Both burst into laughter. Afterwards, they were inseparable.

But it was a very different Mary at sixteen who confided to Clarissa about her pregnancy and her decision to have an abortion on the sly.

"My parents would kill me if they found out," she

moaned. She explained that Rick, the father, had agreed to pay for the operation but threatened to drop her if she had the baby. Rick had been Mary's first serious boyfriend. She was plain. Her mousy brown hair seemed to fall uninspired from her scalp; none of her features attracted any special notice. There was a constant war with an extra five pounds that seemed inexorably drawn to her hips. Rick was a little above her league. He was varsity basketball and friendly with the most popular boys on campus. Mary was moonstruck.

Clarissa had told Mary that she understood her choice. Family Life had already referred Mary to Dr. Jarvis, setting the date, March 5, and arranging to have her picked up from school for a lunch hour abortion that the girls indelicately called "the lunch special." Following "the special," a sympathetic school nurse allowed girls to recover from the "indigestion" on the first aid cot next to her office.

There had been no complications, at least not medical ones. Rick had waited anxiously for Mary's return from the clinic and was visibly relieved to see her enter the school health clinic. But Rick never called her again. Not only did he make sudden changes in direction at Mary's approach, but he began to spread vicious stories about her.

It wasn't just for Rick that Mary pined; even after she had gotten over his cruel and sudden departure, there was yet another emptiness. She was distracted and depressed, and over the months her closeness with Clarissa and everyone else all but dissolved.

A year later in the early morning hours of March 6th, her parents returned from an evening out and found Mary limply draped across her bed in a barbiturate coma. In the ensuing panic, flashing lights, and warbling sirens, Mary was rushed to the hospital where she succumbed to the overdose several hours later. Her mother and father returned home numbed. Two days later, her mother braved Mary's former sanctuary and found the cassette player with a tape tucked under the bed near where her daughter's head had been. Most of the tape was simply the night sounds of their neighborhood—the occasional car, a dog barking. But at the very beginning of the tape were the cryptic words, "One year . . . one year. I'm sorry. I'm sorry. I'm sorry."

The mystery message ground its way though the rumor mill at school for months. If any understood the message, they weren't talking. At first Clarissa saw the implications clearly, but at the prospect of revealing it to her parents . . . well, her conviction diminished. She rationalized that it would serve no useful purpose, and she scrubbed her consciousness clean of the painful memory. Even as Clarissa now paged through her mental memorabilia, there was one carefully excised section. This portion had contained the date of Mary's abortion, the date of her suicide, and the contents of the suicide message.

Clarissa decided to give her period one more week to arrive.

*

Her demand for the end of the menstrual flow still held sway over her mother's body. Her own heart beat rhythmically as daily more and more blood vessels grew to feed the burgeoning additions to her tiny body.

She swam, content in her miniature world. She did not hope for the outside world and her mother's breast. How could she? This was all she wanted. While her mother waited, she grew fingers and toes and wriggled them around.

Already, ominous rumblings threatened from the world that she knew not.

*

"Oh, no!" Clarissa muttered under her breath as she remembered, "I was supposed to get that test a week ago." She mentally chastened herself for letting the year-end business at Mayline interfere with the pregnancy test . . . but the Christmas rush, the Year-End Sale, and preparations for inventory . . . she'd forgotten. "Oh, well, I'll drop into Family Life this afternoon—I'll leave early," she promised. Yet she trembled at the thought of being pregnant.

*

A tremble entered her little world; a flood of tension washed over her body.

*

The afternoon was crisp and cold but unseasonably bright as Clarissa guided her small, imported gas-miser through the after-school traffic starting and stopping its way out of her alma mater. Though she and Matthew both worked, they still suffered the financial constraints of any couple just starting out. The savings of going to Family Life for the test rather than to a private doctor would be substantial. This way the test would be only a blip on their budget; she always bought her pills there anyway, so it would hardly be noticed. She hadn't mentioned her suspicions to Matthew yet in hopes that she wouldn't have to. A visit to the doctor would be a huge neon "look-at-me" sign over the situation. Clarissa was loath to add to his burdens. *Besides,* she thought, *this is the '90s; I'm a grown woman; I can take care of myself.*

Clarissa stowed her car in the narrow space in the lot and strode toward the clean, appealing office building bearing the familiar green Family Life logo, only to be confronted by an older woman who held out a pamphlet and said, "Before you go in there, you should know the truth about that organization."

Clarissa hesitated mid-stride and, as if frozen, stared at the woman. She had already heard about the anti-choice fanatics who screamed insults and shoved people, terrorizing clients of Family Life and patients at Greenbriar. Clarissa had never expected to meet any of them; they were only figures she occasionally saw on the evening news where they were shown in a melee outside Greenbriar. She never wondered why these people were there. It never occurred to her to watch carefully enough to notice who was shoving whom. The tone of the reporters led her, along with most viewers, to assume that it was the anti-abortionists who were to blame.

With this in mind she ducked her head, stiffened her shoulders, and pushed past the woman, leaving her seated on the cold pavement, the literature scattered around her.

She thought she heard the woman call, "Clare!" as the door closed behind her.

*

"Clare! Long time, no see!" the voice rang out in the Family Life waiting room.

Clarissa, still tense from the encounter outside and now vaguely threatened that someone here had recognized her, wheeled around.

"I haven't seen you since I don't know when! Graduation? Wow! What a coincidence seein' you here!"

It was Jennifer Tubbs. She was a high school friend— a friend in that teenage way that you are friends with people who end up at all the same parties and dances and perhaps share some of the same closer friends.

Clarissa remembered that her arrival at Morrow in her sophomore year had been greeted with cracks about her name, especially from the boys. Actually, most came from the less mature boys seeking a way to make contact with the stunning redhead. None of this fazed Jennifer; she knew she was at least in the running as one of the most attractive girls in the school. She couldn't have topped five feet, three inches, but she was slender. Her clear, creamy complexion and her brilliant auburn hair were a great combination.

Jennifer always liked having a good time. She was smart enough to pass her classes with a minimum of work, so she put most of her energy into her social life. By Clarissa's relatively high standards, Jennifer could have been considered promiscuous. But Clarissa did not judge. She knew, as did others, that Jennifer didn't simply sleep around loosely, though she did feel that sex was appropriate in special, close relationships. Besides, she was really careful; she had been "on the pill" since she was fourteen, long before her parents were aware of it. Family Life had obliged her there.

"I just came in to drop off a urine specimen," she said in a stage whisper much louder than Clarissa thought necessary. "Might be PG. I think I screwed up on my pills or sump'm . . . Or maybe I'm just one of the lucky 2 percent, huh? What are *you* up to?"

Clarissa covered her embarrassment. "Well, you

know I married Matthew—you *did* get my invitation, didn't you? Anyway . . ."

"Yeah, yeah, I remember getting it, and I wanted to come, I really did, but—well, you know—my boyfriend had tickets to Acapulco and—you know, and . . ."

"Well, Jen, what have you been doing since high school? Are you married?"

"Married? Not yet. You know me. I've had a lot of friends, done some traveling. But I've kind of settled with Brad, and I'm hoping we'll get hitched. Other than that, I'm not doing much. How about you?"

Clarissa answered with a hint of pride. "I'm working at Mayline downtown . . ."

"Wow, Clare! Mayline!" Jennifer interrupted. "Fancy place. What do you do there—run the place?"

"Hardly. I'm in sales, but I have my sights set on being a buyer. Matthew works at Casco."

"Boy, you *have* been busy. I do feel kind of bad that I didn't make it to your wedding."

"Oh, I understand," Clarissa answered politely.

"So what brings you slumming around here?"

"I just need to get a test myself," Clarissa informed her, hoping Jennifer would probe no further.

"Well, congrats and all that. I just dropped off mine—get the results tomorrow, so I was on my way out. Say, did you run into that lady outside, the one with the pamphlets?"

Clarissa nodded.

"You're not gonna believe this, but that's Mary's mom—Mary Willis's mom!" Clarissa's jaw dropped and Jennifer went on, "Yeah, she really looks different—acts different too. I read one of those things she hands out—claims Family Life supports people being queer and everything. Anyway, she didn't recognize me—been a while, you know—and I didn't know Mary real well. Anyway, then she tells me, she says, 'These people are responsible for my daughter's death.' Can you believe that? Responsible for her death? Anyway, I'm thinking, 'I'm outta here!' So I came in."

The long-buried memories of Mary's death struggled for recognition in Clarissa's mind, but she quashed them.

Jennifer peered out the tinted glass front of the building and continued absently, "I hope she's gone now." Then, glancing at her watch, she exclaimed, "Oh, wow! Look at the time, will ya! Man, I gotta go. Hey, give me your number, maybe we can get together sometime, huh?"

Quickly they exchanged numbers, and Jennifer vanished out the door toward the parking lot.

Clarissa glanced around the pleasantly appointed room, and it seemed that no one had paid any attention to their conversation. She inwardly breathed a sigh and relaxed thinking, *Maybe I'm just paranoid because of that woman making me upset—Mary's Mom? Why did she have to be so pushy?*

The woman behind the mountain of paperwork handed her a specimen jar and a ream of forms, waved toward the door marked "Women" and said, "Leave the specimen in there." Then, as if realizing the harried sound in her voice, she continued more pleasantly, "We'll have the results for you in about two hours, dear, if you care to wait."

Having completed the specimen, Clarissa lowered herself into a Danish-style chair that faced the pastel abstract wall mural and absently picked up a copy of an old *Ms.* magazine. She'd already read most of this issue, and she absorbed nothing of the remaining articles that she scanned as her tension mounted. Just when she was beginning to question the wisdom of waiting for the results, the

25

nurse stepped through the aperture and intoned, "Mzzz Strausssss."

As Clarissa looked up, the nurse beckoned. Clarissa followed her into the close counseling cubicle replete with cutesy posters of animals embossed with popular truisms or warm, fuzzy sentiments. On the wall beside the desk was a bulletin board prominently featuring flyers with every conceivable variation on the "female" symbol—the circle with the attached cross.

"I'm Carol," the woman said as she rounded her desk, appearing to be headed for a much-practiced landing in her tan swivel chair. "The earliest I can set you up at Dr. Jarvis's would be, let's see, a week from today. How does that sound to you?"

Clarissa was speechless. The nurse hadn't even read the forms. She had simply assumed that Clarissa was single, that she was in trouble, and that she wanted an abortion. "I'll have to think about it," she said faintly.

Carol ushered her out of the room saying, "Don't wait too long. You're about eight weeks, if your form is correct, and you don't want to wait for the second trimester if you can help it."

The others seated in the waiting room were a blur, not even registering in her agitated mind as she passed by the literature rack and out the front door. The sight of Mrs. Willis, busy with another victim, served only to speed her escape. The rhetoric of abortion spoke of "a woman's choice" and "her own body," but she told herself she wanted to make this decision with Matthew.

Her mind drove the car more by autopilot than by conscious effort, her thoughts paralyzed by a flood of hormones produced by agitation. She could not admit to herself yet that she had already decided the fate of her child. She hid behind a mask of indecisiveness.

*

It was similar to what she'd felt before, but with greater intensity. The flood of hormones crossing the placental barrier brought a sudden wave of undirected fear. Of what, in this normally secure world?

At eight weeks gestation, all her systems were functioning, quite an accomplishment for someone who was a mere spark six short weeks ago. Daily, she had celebrated life, darting from one edge of her private universe to the next. Though her brain had been functioning for some time, the EEG would be able to pick it up in about a week.

But now this tension. This was the first time that the capital "H" had been taken out of "Home." There was no command she could issue to resolve this distress; she was helpless. The threatening cloud was gathering in the wider world outside, but she could not understand that.

*

Clarissa came to self-awareness seated behind the wheel of the car in her driveway, the engine still clattering under the hood. She shook herself, cut the motor, and eased out of the vehicle. She followed the curved walk to the porch of the modest, ranch-style home they were renting. Nothing in particular stood out about this house except the fresh tan and white paint job that Matthew had just completed. The colors had not been Clarissa's choice, but her favorites would have necessitated special mixing, an expense the landlord eschewed.

Walking inside, Clarissa glanced into the dining room and spotted the crisp, folded sheet of paper rising like a pup tent from the surface of the mahogany table, her name printed across its face in that artistic, but Spartan hand of Matthew's.

The name could have been typed, and she would have known its source. Matthew, in typical style, was the only one who called her "Clarissa." It was a comic scene whenever they attended the occasional "client-softener" parties at her father-in-law's grand hilltop home. Matthew would say, ". . . and this is my wife, Clarissa. She . . ." At that point, she would gracefully extend her hand and interrupt, "Call me Clare." In the beginning, this irritated Matthew, but it had since become one of their private jokes: The Introduction Ritual, they had dubbed it.

Clarissa unfolded the slice of company stationery with the distinctive Casco logo embossed on the top. She could visualize Matthew hunched over the table writing the summary in his abbreviated style. His larger frame was ill-designed to fit the off-the-rack suits they could afford. Perhaps when they were doing better financially, custom tailored suits would be possible. Matthew was not particularly handsome, his straw-colored hair in a continual state of disarray and his close-set, pale blue eyes, the color of cornflowers, somewhat small for his broad face. But it had been Matthew's persistence and determination that had won her heart.

The note explained, in brief, that he had been called by his father to Washington, DC, to bring additional expertise to his dad's renegotiating of a Pentagon contract. Casco produced cast and injection molded parts for everything from widgets to warheads; they were a small firm, highly reputed for the unmatched precision of their parts.

Matthew went on to say that he'd tried to call her at Mayline that afternoon, only to find she had gone. He would be back in a week. "Call you tonight. Love, Matthew."

2 THE EDGE OF THE BATTLEFIELD

Dr. Elgin (his friends called him Bud) Tower was five feet, ten inches, muscular, and black—very black. There was a sprinkling of gray in the close-cropped hair. His easy grin, often appearing more like a smirk at some secret insight about life, immediately disarmed the people he met. This appearance belied the harder realities that daily confronted him in the coarse underbelly of the world where he functioned. His counseling practice was successful. His patients responded well to the confrontational method that he called "nouthetic," from the Greek word meaning "to admonish."

But wherever there is success, critics abound; many other professionals said, not quite jokingly, that Bud had graduated from the John Wayne School of Psychology (Quit yer blubberin' and act like a man!). But everyone who met him sensed his genuine concern for others. His direct approach came out of that concern; he was certain it was the best way to the root of personal issues.

He noticed his "rogue" file in the drawer of the file cabinet as he searched for the next patient's file. It reminded him of his other claim to fame, or notoriety. The newspaper clips inside marked his relatively new yet luminous career as a lawbreaker—a catalog of arrests at the local abortion clinic.

Bud smirked as he looked at a clip and remembered the first arrest at Greenbriar. He had walked boldly past the wide-eyed clinic escorts. "Just doing my job as a counselor," he said into their astonished faces as he strode into the waiting room. Bud now laughed at the simplicity of that first "rescue." *How many times has he been arrested ?* he asked himself in mock seriousness. *Only his court reporter knows for sure.* Already he had served two thirty-day maximum sentences in the county lock-up, but, undeterred and unrepentant, he merely began to counsel the men within those concrete walls. There was a returned wayward husband as well as a struggling gas jockey—formerly a car thief—and now a full-time evangelist to show for his efforts.

The memory of these two "losers" brought a chuckle. Occasionally, the gas jockey/evangelist would drop by his office to see "the Doc." And he still saw the reunited couple weekly at church.

Bud had been "asleep at the switch" when the 1973 *Roe v. Wade* decision of the U. S. Supreme Court legalized abortion during all nine months of pregnancy. The court had decided the legal issue with no regard for the medical facts and certainly with no thought of the psychological consequences to the woman. Bud recalled the stylishly dressed, dark-haired professional woman who later had marched into his office looking for prescription sleeping tablets, though she disguised the request with broad hints.

Bud said bluntly, "I'm sorry, I don't use drugs in therapy unless there is absolutely no choice. You don't want a cure, you want a pacifier."

An astonished look crossed her face, and then anger. "Well, . . . I . . . I didn't . . ."

Bud held up his hand. "Don't be offended. Sit down and tell me what this is all about. You're paying for an hour; you may as well get your money's worth."

She sat and began to cry. When she relaxed her guard, the stress was etched deeply on her face. "I can't sleep. I lie awake, night after night. I am so tired at work I'm afraid I'll lose my job. I feel like I am coming apart."

"Why can't you sleep?" Bud probed.

"I have these dreams, nightmares actually, of babies crying . . . or dying, of finding dead babies or hiding dead babies. It's horrible!"

Bud was puzzled. He struggled to recall what he had read in a study some time before. In fact he had read several articles about women suffering these symptoms. He suddenly grasped the situation. "So you've had an abortion?"

She gave him a startled look. "Yes. Yes, I have."

It was the last appointment for the day, so Bud listened to her long after the traditional fifty minutes were up.

After that, he began to pay particular attention to some seemingly unconnected symptoms in his other patients. *If there are one and a half million abortions a year,* he thought to himself, *and even two-thirds are first timers, that is a potential of a million new cases—a million new walking time bombs—each year since 1973.*

Before long, women suffering from the now familiar Post-traumatic Stress Disorder often seen in Vietnam War vets inundated his practice. Bud's persistent investigative work confirmed that "Vietnam" for these women was an abortion table.

The symptoms were so predictable that Bud was staggered. It was several years after *Roe v. Wade* before the psychiatric literature dared mention Postabortion Syndrome and Postabortion Suicide, but the professional associations still refused to accept the glaring facts. Even highly placed pro-life scientists were cowed into denial.

The details differed from patient to patient, but there were many similarities. Dreams were normally the first stage. After these came depression, intrusive memories of the abortion, diminished interest in friends and important activities, sleep disturbance, and reduced capacity for emotional involvement.

Bud began to understand the deep, self-inflicted wounds these women had from their abortions. This trauma, he soon found, was not limited to the women who had had abortions. Many nurses who assisted in abortions and doctors who performed them also experienced it.

Bud had done volunteer counseling one day a week at nearby Morrow High School for several years. He remembered clearly when these same symptoms began appearing in students as well. He knew then it was time for action.

With characteristic thoroughness, he spent several months studying abortion from every possible angle—legal, moral, philosophical, and medical. Meanwhile, he began to support pro-life organizations financially. He attended pickets and lent a hand at sidewalk counseling. When he stood up at a PTA meeting and spoke of the "Family Life/Greenbriar clinic duet that played the dance of death for these young women and their babies," people exchanged startled glances. That speech and others that followed made a number of people nervous.

Then Bud did the unpardonable. A sophomore sat in his school office one day and twisted her long blonde hair as she launched into what was now a familiar story.

"I'm . . . pregnant," she whispered. "And I'm scared

to death of what my parents will say." She told him about her situation.

"You simply *must* begin to take responsibility for your own actions," he had told her. "Give that baby a home—preferably your own or, if need be, somebody else's."

When the young woman's mother heard about this advice, she suffered an attack of what Bud called the Post-Bra-Burning Latent Feminist Syndrome. She called the newspaper, and the next morning the headlines cried, "He's Brainwashed My Daughter!" The girl was taken to a "proper" counselor, after which she made the "proper" decision; she aborted her child. Some pro-life picketers present that day claimed she was virtually dragged into Greenbriar. Mom, still in the throes of the Syndrome, screamed that she would sue the school district to recover the costs of the "proper" counselor and for mental anguish and for violation of civil rights and . . .

The school board cried "Uncle!" before the first form was filed, before the first letter-of-intent. The board announced that it would no longer accept Dr. Tower's voluntary services. Boiling down all their rhetoric, Bud knew the real reason was because he had neglected to promote to a pregnant teen her "right" to kill her unborn child.

"They, too," Bud said, "are sufferers of the Latent Feminist Syndrome."

It was shortly after his untimely departure from Morrow that Bud picked up his newspaper, and a headline caught his eye: "Local Teen Commits Suicide." It was a Morrow student, Mary Willis. He remembered her as a girl in transit from adolescence to adulthood. He'd never counseled with her, though he was aware of how badly she needed it. The paper trail of Mary's "lunch special" ran across his desk. He saw reports of troubling symptoms. Rather than the usual drop in grades, however, Mary's grades improved. Everything else in her life had dropped out, and she concentrated all her efforts on her studies; a classic escape from her own thoughts.

"Everyone entering the Greenbriar Clinic when I am sidewalk counseling bears Mary's face," Bud told his pastor. "Pro-lifers act as the baby's 'champion,' but it's still the baby against the abortionist. When the abortionist wins, a baby dies; when the baby wins, the abortionist goes on killing anyway. But the death and bloodshed are real."

"I'm not sure what you are driving at," the pastor replied. "You seem torn up over it. What is it you think you can do?"

"You're right, I am torn up," Bud responded. "This is a war, and the clinic property line is the edge of the battle zone. Greenbriar is a haunt of bloodthirsty demons and their human dupes."

So the act of walking past the gawking faces of the escorts into the very throat of hell—through the clinic doors—that first time had seemed inevitable. Inside, the atmosphere was thick with panic and desperation, belying the polished-wood, hanging-fern atmosphere the clinic tried to project.

Bud had squatted down next to the nearest patient and began to plead for the baby's life. "My name is Dr. Tower, and I'm a counselor," he began. "I realize this is a difficult time for you, but you need to reconsider this decision. You already sense something wrong, and you won't feel any better about it if you go through with it in that state of mind. You don't really want to kill that little baby inside, do you?"

Moments later, an officer, shaking Bud's shoulder and asking him to leave, invaded his consciousness. "You have to leave," the voice insisted, "or I'll have to arrest you."

But all Bud could see was the softening heart through the eyes of the woman before him. He felt it would be a great sin of omission to leave her half convinced, so he ignored the patrolman's demand. *Just a few more words and she'll leave,* he thought. "Listen, you can come here any time, but once you've done the abortion you can't decide over again. It becomes permanent history for both you and the baby."

The lone officer, young and inexperienced, was confused by Tower's disregard for his authority. He went to call for assistance; Bud was not a small man.

But when the woman abruptly rose and bolted from the clinic into the waiting arms of the sidewalk counselors outside, the clinic director began to shriek, "Arrest that man! Stop him right now. I'll sue the whole police department if you don't."

Already Bud was talking to another interested woman. Dollars were being lost here!

Bud wasn't going anywhere. He did not resist, but neither did he help; he simply refused to move. The policeman put him in cuffs, but that did not stop him from calling to the women, "You really don't want to do this. I'm a professional counselor, and you don't know how badly this will affect you—not to mention your baby."

By the time he was dragged bodily across the polished hardwood floor of the anteroom, there were eight squad cars and a paddy wagon parked out front. Blue and red lights whirling and bright yellow police-line tape strewn across every tree and bush created the atmosphere of a riot zone. The cameras of the four local TV stations were rolling, recording the melee and finally coming to rest on the quiet man being carried head first out the oaken door, down the steps, and into the waiting van. The quiet man smiled; three women had left the clinic, babies intact.

∗

Until then, the local pro-life movement had written letters, demonstrated, passed out literature, picketed, marched, declared, pleaded, cajoled, and prayed—but never trespassed. Bud's solo rescue hit the community with a crash.

The feminists and the press cried "Foul!" and a parade of visitors appeared at his door.

"The *News-Clarion* called you a terrorist," challenged the WCRF newsman.

"Who, exactly, was terrorized—the clinic's accountant?" countered Ben.

"The clinic director put your violent trespassing on a par with mad clinic bombers. He claimed you were trained in a secret terrorist camp."

"I was only obeying Scripture. The book of Proverbs tells us to rescue those being dragged to slaughter."

Bud also found himself the subject of controversy in the pro-life ranks.

"How could you do that?" asked a local leader. "We're trying to educate people and change the laws. You will destroy the hard work of many years with this radical stuff."

"But you did all that work without regard for the babies who are dying today. During each of those 'years of work' a million and a half babies died," Bud replied. "How many more will die before the law is changed?"

Most of the furor was predictable. Groups that focused on legal changes only, such as the local "evangelical think tank," denounced the rescue mission as "the equivalent of the violence inside the clinic."

But the maelstrom also stirred up a cadre of people who wanted to do more. They had heard of others in the country doing direct action, had read about all the different methods and means, but it never seriously occurred to them to do the same. Bud's ground-breaking move—especially when the results became known—gave birth to a small rescue movement.

At first, the dividing line between his supporters and detractors seemed to harden. But then the judge handed Bud a thirty-day sentence, adding the order, "No work release; no early release." This was in the face of a crowded county jail system that regularly released serious offenders for lack of space. Suddenly, there was a small exodus to Bud's side.

In time about six people came to comprise the core of the local rescue movement, and perhaps another fifty became "rescue supporters." On certain occasions, there were as many as fifteen rescuers. Some would participate once or twice and then continue in other pro-life work. They tried many methods—blocking the entrances, occupying the procedure rooms—but Bud preferred just going in and talking to the women personally. Always, the rescuers insisted on strict nonviolence.

Bud's detractors were many. So he began his defense by giving them Melanie Block's phone number. Melanie had come for an abortion about a year ago, only to find Bud and his cohorts blocking the door.

"You have no right to do this," she declared angrily.

"Please reconsider your decision," Bud replied. "Abortion kills a human being."

She left the porch to fume, not to reconsider. But Bud was surprised when six months later a woman came up to him in front of the clinic, gently carrying a small bundle.

"Hello. You won't remember me, but I want to thank you." She unfolded the blanket from her bundle to reveal a tiny pink face topped with thick black hair. "This is

Carol. She's the joy of my life, and you're tó blame. You stopped me from aborting her six months ago. I'm afraid I didn't have the courage to name her Bud though."

Melanie was only too happy to tell people Bud sent her way, "The rescuers say it's murder, and their actions back up what they say. They cared enough to risk arrest to save me and my baby."

Weekly pickets continued. These seemed to help convey the idea to the women that there was something wrong going on inside. Bud appeared in front of Greenbriar several times a week, setting off warning buzzers inside the clinic. When would the next invasion come?

*

On this particular bitter-cold, late January morning, the dense clouds barely revealing the muddy light of sunrise, Bud sighted a woman hunkered down and walking furtively toward the clinic. She had rounded the corner two blocks away, streamers of red hair swinging as she walked, and caught sight of the picketers. Their placards declared, "Jesus loves you," and, "Abortion is murder," block-printed over a poster-size photo of a mangled baby. Bud could tell by the way her gait faltered that she felt there was no prudent retreat. When she arrived where Bud stood, she pretended she was just a passerby. "What's going on?" she asked.

"This is an abortion clinic, ma'am," he answered. "The decision to come here has serious consequences. This will explain some of them." He handed her some literature.

She would not have recognized Tower from his picture in the paper. He was a few years and many gray hairs beyond that photo. But she had seen him on campus at Morrow years ago, so his face was vaguely familiar.

Just then an escort shoved Ben out of the way and took the woman by the arm saying, "Here, let me help you past this person! You don't need to listen to his lies!"

"Hey! Let go of me," the redhead cried. She jerked her arm free, turned on her heel, and fled down the street from whence she had come.

As the girl disappeared around the corner, Bud silently thanked God and turned to face the angry eyes of the clinic escort.

"Pig!" she spat under her breath before she headed to the two-story colonial house-turned-clinic with the simple legend over the door: Greenbriar Surgicenter.

You need to control yourself, Joan Risner thought as she returned to the clinic. Joan knew Bud, but not as Bud. She'd had to testify against him on several occasions for his clinic invasions. She steamed at the memory. "It is one thing for him to present his point of view," she had testified. "It is quite another to actually prevent people from exercising a legal right by blocking the entrance to the clinic."

She felt that even the terms anti-choicers used were deceptive—rescues, sidewalk counseling. It deeply disturbed Joan that in a nation claiming plurality and tolerance, it was legal to harass people who were exercising their rights. When she had gotten her own abortion several years ago, she had almost changed her mind because of the pickets and the smooth, hypnotic voice of Dr. Tower. She had been "rescued" all right—rescued from the lying, fear-mongering anti-choicers. Her subsequent experiences with the man consisted of the court appearances and snatching unsuspecting women away from him. The only thing that bothered her now was the recurring dream of a crying baby which she could not find. *And I wouldn't have that problem,* she thought, *if it weren't for this paternalistic society and its religious guilt trips designed to keep women "in their place."*

Yet underlying her anger with Tower was a nagging realization. *Put an Afro on that man,* Joan thought, *and lose about ten years, and he'd be Dr. James Lester.* Lester had been a math professor at the exclusive Eastern college to which Joan had wrangled entrance. He was the only black professor on staff, and she was one of two women in the advanced math program he taught. A quick relationship developed and, in their zeal to protect their liberal college standing, the students and faculty overlooked the usual taboo on student-faculty romances. Had they both been white, things might have been different.

Joan was reluctant to openly admit that the resemblance between Tower and Lester was more than physical. Lester was also an intelligent and passionate man in the social issues. He had championed civil rights as a young man in marches and bus rides in the South. He was the least chauvinistic male she had ever met.

But as time went on, she began to see that his passion hadn't the cutting edge she had hoped for. She was more than a little disappointed. His social conscience had become "mainstream."

It came to a head when the women's studies department was supporting the addition of "sexual orientation" to the list of protected minorities at the college. "There is no evidence that homosexuals have been discriminated against by the college," Lester argued. "In fact, their enrollment has been encouraged."

"That's beside the point," Joan said. "Some gay men have been assaulted on campus, and the college owes them a show of support."

"Hey," he answered, "there is nothing to indicate that those assaults were motivated by homophobia. Actually, all the evidence shows the motive to be simple robbery. The gays have the same right to protection from both campus and city police as anyone else. Assault is assault—whether against gays or straights. The law will prosecute."

"You actually believe that they'll get the same consideration as straights?"

"In this town, yes."

"So you think their rights will be protected by the system. I thought you, of all people, would be aware that civil rights must be taken. 'Go through the system'—you should be able to see the fallacy of that."

Now, she realized that she had simply not been able to forgive him his humanity. Somehow she had expected, without realizing it was a stereotype, that his blackness would make him more passionate about people's rights—more—more something! She was embarrassed now to realize that this expectation was akin to believing his blackness would endow him with greater sexual prowess. Her liberal upbringing had armored her against such obvious prejudices but had failed to protect her from this more subtle stereotyping.

The difference between Tower and Lester was that Tower was still passionate outside the mainstream—though his chosen issues reflected, in her view, a Neanderthal ethic.

*

Joan surveyed the streets from the clinic's top step, ready to swoop down to deliver any prey from the clutches of the fanatics. No clients were in sight.

She glanced back through the five-foot oval of

beveled glass in the oak door and saw the waiting room half full of women. *This has got to be better than those lethal back-alley days,* she thought. She frowned at the wire mesh over the beautiful antique door. The clinic had felt compelled to cover this treasure and all the lower story windows as well. No one could predict what the anti-choice forces might do. She thought, *There'll be hell to pay if there's ever a fire here.*

A brown Toyota slowed as it passed in front of the clinic, the woman inside craning her neck to see the sign. Joan recognized the look and, knowing that the woman would have to park about a block down the street, left the porch and walked briskly in that direction. Normally, she and the other escorts tried to work in pairs, but they were shorthanded on this murky Saturday morning. There were only three; one was in the back getting cups of coffee to bring out for herself and Joan; the other was helping the most recent client check in at the desk. She could see the Toyota backing into a slot and two of the harassment squad headed that direction.

*

After the confrontation with Joan, Bud had wandered up toward the clinic where the picketers patiently paced back and forth. Several chatted amiably as they walked. Two sidewalk counselors were down the street from where Bud had just come, with two more in the opposite direction. Greenbriar was located in the center of a long block in an older residential area. The neighbors disliked the commotion of the picket line, and they were not exactly thrilled with the clinic being there either. They vacillated between blaming the clinic and blaming the pro-lifers for their woes. They were locked into their homes; no one would buy houses in that area because of the pickets and the clinic business traffic. How the clinic had gotten the zoning exemption so quietly was a matter of much speculation. The clinic didn't seem to need to meet fire safety regulations either.

One of the picketers limped toward Bud. "Hey, Bud, are you going to make the March for Life next month?" Mark Schmalz had just recently become involved in pro-life activities. His limp resulted from a childhood bout with polio.

"I sure hope so. It really depends on what Judge Tovelli has to say in my hearing; I've also got a probation violation hearing on the twelfth."

"I'm trying to get some time off work to attend. I'll try to be there."

"Thanks, Mark, it's always good to see friendly faces in the courtroom," Bud said.

"Say," Mark asked, "I'm kind of new at all this court stuff, but isn't there some kind of law that says that if you break a law, it's okay if you had a good reason . . . you know, you were trying to accomplish something better?"

"That's right," Bud replied smiling. "It's called Choice of Evils. It's a legal defense, and it means that while you technically broke the law, you were trying to prevent a greater evil than the law itself was designed to prevent—a choice of evils—the lesser of two evils. We've tried to use that defense, but the judges won't allow us."

"What? Even if you can show them an actual baby whose life was saved?"

"That's right, Mark. Even then. It's amazing in a country where one is supposed to be innocent until proven guilty that a man can be denied the use of a legal defense—denied the ability to display his innocence."

The conversation continued, but part of Bud's attention wandered to the clinic porch. He had thought he might go in again today should the opportunity present itself. And it looked as though it might. Bud saw Joan quickly descend the steps and head up the street, leaving the porch unoccupied.

"Excuse me, Mark." Bud moved quickly up the walk, bounded up the stairs, and in a twinkling was inside the clinic. He chose a girl who looked about thirteen; she wore jeans and a pink turtleneck sweater and clutched nervously at the arms of the chair.

As he approached her and lowered himself to meet her eye to eye, the front door swung wide to reveal an incensed Joan Risner, red-faced and hollering, "Tower, you . . ." Mid-stride across the room, her boot went out from under her. Her right foot went forward, and she came down about three quarters of the way to doing a split. Her torso pitched over sideways, slamming her head into an end table.

For a moment no one moved; the silence buzzed in Bud's head. He quickly slid over to her side, checking breathing and pulse; they were present, but she was either stunned or unconscious. "Call a doctor!" he said automatically, knowing that there was one on the premises.

The clinic director rushed into the room, pushed Bud away with her foot, and said, "Leave her alone. Haven't you done enough?" Dr. Piper, one of Jarvis's hirelings, came in just as Joan's blue eyes opened. The doctor told her to lie still.

Bud moved away and began to talk to the young girl in the pink sweater again. The girl was shaken. She turned to Bud and said, "Help me get out of here." Bud took her by the arm and led her out the door. A police car and the ambulance arrived simultaneously as they hit the bottom step of the porch. Patrolman Jim Davis stepped out of his prowl car, his lanky frame rising to its full height, and called, "Hol' it, Tower!" Davis charged his partner with holding Bud while he led the protesting girl back into the clinic. After half an hour, the overzealous officer released her, satisfied that she was leaving of her own free will. Then he turned his attention to Bud.

"When're you gonna give this up, Tower?" Davis drawled. "You're just wastin' valuable po-lice time. I could be catchin' real bad-guys."

"I'm not stopping you," Bud grinned. "Go ahead. I'll just go back and save more babies. In fact, that's what you should be doing . . ."

Davis cut him off. "All right, all right, we been through all this b'fore. You know the pr'cedure. Downtown, write'chu a ticket and cut'cha loose." Davis swung wide the rear door of the blue and white patrol car.

Officer James Davis would not be drawn into conversation during the short cruise back to the precinct station. The patrolman's red face revealed the dammed-up words awaiting release from behind the clenched teeth and tightened jaw. Davis had arrested this malefactor before and was "about up to here with these fanatics." His partner, following the other man's lead, remained mute.

The squad car rolled casually into the cavern leading to the underground garage of the station and swung into the vacant slot near the door marked "Booking."

Bud's eyes were still adjusting to the subterranean darkness as he skootched out along the fiberglass bench in the rear of the car, scraping his manacled hands along the back of the seat. He stood without assistance and was led into the brilliant fluorescent glow coming from above the now-familiar booking desk.

"Hey, Tomás!" Bud called, recognizing Tom Mendoza behind the massive oak partition of the desk.

Tom glanced up from his smattering of papers, rolled his eyes, and sighed, "You? Again?"

"Hey, I'm only trying to protect lives—which, by the way, is also your job. Isn't that what it says on the side of your cars, 'To protect and serve'?"

Davis's partner, Jack, finally spoke up. "I thought you were supposed to be a Christian. Aren't Christians supposed to obey the law?"

"Son," Bud countered, "are *you* a Christian?"

"Well—uh—yeah. Yes—I am."

"That's good!" Bud grinned. "And you, Mendoza, I know you're a practicing Catholic, right?"

Tom nodded.

"How about you, Davis? You a Christian?" Bud queried looking squarely into the policeman's angry face.

"Course I am!" he spat in return.

"Well, then," Bud rolled on as though at home in the place, "it is the Christian's duty to obey God when governments enact laws consistent with God's character or that at least don't violate His commands. But the Word of God commands us to open our mouths for the mute and for the rights of the unfortunate, to defend the rights of the afflicted and needy. Who's more mute and afflicted than a preborn baby about to be slaughtered?"

"That's all well and good," interrupted Mendoza, "but we have a job to do; we're supposed to be good employees. We don't make the laws; we just enforce them. And abortion is the law."

"But whose law?"

Jim Davis rounded the end of the booking table and stood with the other two officers. It was a perfect picture of the conflict—the table dividing their points of view as much as their bodies. Jim, controlling his pitch and volume, strained out the words, "Lissen, bein' against abortion is one thing. I think all of us here are against abortion, but the way you go about it makes us all look like jackasses. It's to the point where a lot'a us won't even express our 'pinion on the subject 'cause people 'sociate us with weirdos like you. That's what sticks in my craw. You self-righteous, holier-than-thou fanatics screaming and harassing people—then breaking the law—and telling everyone that they aren't really against abortion if they don't do things your way. It's your tactics I object to, Mister! We're simply on opposite sides of the fence."

It was a long speech for the normally slow-talking cop. He settled back.

"Really?" Bud quizzed, carefully leveling his gaze directly at Davis and then at each of the others in turn. "Then what side of the fence is the abortionist on?"

For a moment the three officers teetered between rage and embarrassment and finally took refuge in the formality of officialdom by filling out forms and handing Bud his summons. He was unceremoniously ejected onto the street.

"Dr. Tower!" the voice of Mark Schmalz rose over the din of traffic. "I came down to give you a lift back to your car."

"Thanks," Tower replied. "Could we stop at a phone booth on the way? I need to call the hospital."

Bud tried to find out how Joan was doing; he called her home, but her roommates wouldn't say anything. The hospital had treated her and planned to keep her overnight for observation, but beyond that, he drew a blank.

3 THE LINE IS DRAWN

Clarissa spent that first night alone—alone with the knowledge that she was pregnant. "I can't talk over something this important on the phone," she said aloud to herself. So when she heard Matthew's quiet voice over the receiver, she said nothing about the matter. "Oh, hello, Matthew. How was the flight?"

Matthew was perceptive; he thought she seemed distant. *Perhaps she is angry over my sudden departure,* he thought. "Is anything wrong?" he asked aloud anxiously at several points in the conversation. The exchange was less than satisfying, considering this was their first separation.

The rest of the evening, Clarissa's thoughts performed a three-ring circus in her mind—whirling, twirling thoughts without a center. *A baby now would really interfere with my life—our lives,* she corrected. *This is so—inconvenient.* Sitting in the dark living room, looking at the silhouette of the corner table and lamp before the moon-washed curtains over the rear window, the first conscious hint of her decision tentatively surfaced.

*

She felt some relief from tension, but there was still a constant, underlying contraction of the muscles. Clarissa's daughter began adjusting to the tightness. Her formidable opponent reared its monstrous head in the mind of her own mother, but she knew it not.

Regaining some of her former contentment, she sucked at her fist and snuggled for sleep in the crook between her mother's backbone and pelvis. Mother wouldn't notice her two-inch presence there.

*

Clarissa awoke groggily, with anxiety hanging over from the late night and her pumped up adrenal system. The bleak morning sky did nothing to inspire her to show up at Mayline. She briefly considered skipping her morning workout, but realized that such were the beginnings of an abandoned regimen. She steeled herself against the chilling, blustering turbulence that struck her as she exited the house for the five-mile run. The neighborhood passed her eyes unnoticed as her running mind began warming up for a day of distressful thoughts. Already the turmoil of the night before was beginning to press upon her. Clarissa came to abrupt awareness at the squall of a horn and the high-pitched protest of car tires skidding across the pavement under a ton and a half of steel. In her preoccupation, she quickly dismissed the close call and sped home for a shower and preparation for work.

Today was the first day of inventory, so there was no need to look like a fashion plate, but Clarissa instinctively knew the importance of always looking the part she hoped to play. So she selected a simple but tasteful navy suit that made her appear all business. The final touch, her hair in a bun, completed the image.

Again she stepped out into the gray morning just as the shifting breeze shot up to a crescendo, scattering some of fall's leftover leaves onto the porch. Holding some stray hairs in place, she hurried to the driveway where she had left the car. As she swung open the door of the burgundy Datsun, she spotted Mrs. Frank next door on her daily trek to retrieve the carelessly tossed newspaper. "Hi, Mrs. Frank!" she said with a genuine smile.

"Hello," the older woman said with evident surprise. "It's a little early for you, isn't it?"

"Nothing is too early in the world of women's fashion," Clarissa joked. Then she added, "We're doing inventory the next three days."

Picking the paper out of the tam junipers that bordered the front of her house, Mrs. Frank asked, "How's Matthew doing? I haven't seen him lately."

"Flew to Washington, DC! Company business with the military. He'll be back next week."

Mrs. Frank frowned sympathetically. "Oh, that's too bad. I'll bet you miss him. Well, I better let you get out of this awful wind. Good-bye!"

Clarissa thought, *You have no idea how much I've missed him.* She slid in behind the steering wheel, cranked over the engine, and backed out of the driveway. She wondered how Mrs. Frank always looked so fresh (in her housewifely way), especially with six kids. The woman was always pleasant, always thinking of others.

Big splotches of rain obscured her windshield as she piloted the aging Datsun down the freeway. Flicking on the wipers, she looked up to the sign on the back of the bus ahead: "Family Life Association—caring professionals in times of need." The notice brought all the unpleasantness of the presumptuous nurse back again. Clarissa rehashed the incident, growing angry at the recollection.

The spatter had turned to a downpour by the time she wheeled into the downtown parking structure. Mentally, she blessed Providence that Mayline had reserved space in this high-rise parking garage. "At least I won't come in drenched," she sighed with relief as she left the Datsun and headed for the Mayline rear entrance.

Clarissa was met at the door by Nancy Scott, the tall, rawboned blonde who handled everything from stock to accounting and billing for the store. Today she wore her hair in braids, which enhanced the Valkyrie appearance she normally projected. Already, Nancy was sorting through the racks, checking tags, and noting lot numbers. Myrna, Clarissa's boss, assigned the two to work together because of Nancy's greater familiarity with the stock. Clarissa hung up her coat, picked up the clipboard, and asked, "Where do I start?"

The detail work consumed her thoughts for several hours. Around noon Clarissa and Nancy dropped into the chairs in the employees' corner of the stockroom and pulled out their lunches. Clarissa drew out an apple and a small plastic bag with carrot sticks. Nancy opened a bag to reveal a cheese sandwich and a can of diet pop.

"Whew!" Clarissa sighed, "I never realized how tiring that work was."

"Is!" replied Nancy cheerfully, mopping her brow and firing up a cigarette. "Is tiring!"

"At least it helps me take my mind off of Matthew. He's in Washington, DC, for a week or so," Clarissa added.

"Takes your mind off *everything*," Nancy concluded. "DC, huh? Have him bring back some hot air as a memento. It's no wonder you miss him though—he's quite a hunk. My husband was nothing like that man you've got. Yours seems like a real gentleman. When my old man started slapping me around, I booted his butt out the door. *Him* I don't miss."

She leaned back in her chair, took a bite of her sandwich, and dragged a section of the paper from the low coffee table. Squinting at the front page for a moment, she tossed it back as though she had been burned. "Oh, yuk!" she said, "Did you see that? Someone claims to have found little torn-apart babies' bodies in the trash behind that abortion clinic, you know, the one in the Greenbriar district. Yuk!"

Clarissa looked at the headline and the first paragraph. "That's impossible," she said. "They wouldn't just throw them in the trash. Besides, they aren't babies yet anyway, just blobs of tissue."

"Well, they don't show any pictures here, but I've seen pictures of those aborted babies before, and they're more than blobs of tissue. Abortion is bad enough, but trashing the bodies . . . yuk! I hate to think about it."

Clarissa felt defensive. "I think a woman has a right to choose. I'm not sure I would want an abortion either, but sometimes there is no choice. I mean, after all, what about rape victims?"

"But no one has absolute rights—especially when it takes the life of another person. Why, I can't even smoke some places because . . . oops! You don't smoke, do you? I'll put this out . . . sorry."

Nancy found an old soda can and ground out the offending weed. "Anyway, even rape doesn't justify killing the baby . . . what did the baby do wrong? We need to stop rapists, not kill babies. The so-called hard cases are only a small percentage of abortions—most abortions are for convenience anyway. Pure selfishness! I'm not a real religious person, but I figure wrong is wrong, and somehow we're going to pay for all this stuff."

Clarissa's unadmitted decision to have an abortion strengthened at Nancy's mention of "convenience"; her anger rose to the surface. "Well, I'm not in a position to judge others," she replied icily. "And lots of religious people, including the pastor of my church, aren't so black-and-white about right and wrong."

Nancy suddenly realized she had offended. "I'm sorry," she said softly. "I didn't mean to come off as self-righteous or trivialize the issue. Hope I didn't hurt your feelings or something." But she could see by Clarissa's expression that she had hit a tender spot.

Clarissa threw, "It's okay," at Nancy and went back to work. They hardly talked to each other for the rest of the day.

*

She was developing the tiny loops and whorls of the individual fingerprints she would bear throughout her life. She sped from side to side in her watery world, jumped, started at a sudden loud sound, and hiccuped.

Outside, the hostilities escalated.

*

The next two days of inventory came and went. Clarissa brooded over the complications a baby would bring. It would virtually end her career hopes, coming at the beginning of her tenure at Mayline. Mayline didn't have a maternity department; their clientele would hardly be interested in "that sort of thing." Even with her and Matthew both working, their financial position was nothing to write home about. They had really wanted to have substantial equity in a larger home, the furniture paid off, a newer car, and the income for a private preschool before a child came. Nancy's comment about "convenience" stung her conscience. No matter how she rephrased her objections to this pregnancy in her own mind, her reasonings kept reading back as "convenience." The very sight of Nancy caused color to rush to her face.

After inventory, Clarissa, feigning illness, claimed the next two days off. She knew that taking sick time was not politic this early in her employment, but she felt she needed the time to sort things out. Consciously, she still maintained that she would make this decision with Matthew; actually, she had already decided. But Nancy's comment rankled in her mind. *Who does she think she is,* Clarissa fumed inwardly, *judging other people?*

*

Clarissa's daughter snoozed comfortably, rocking in the amniotic fluid. She stirred faintly as some disturbance invaded her prenatal dreams. At ten weeks, machines could register the brain activity associated with those dreams, but not what a preborn baby would dream.

Her mother had decided her fate, but the war for her life was not yet over.

*

"Clare? Is that you?"

Clarissa recognized the voice of Jennifer Tubbs on the receiver. "Yes, it's me."

"Hey, my test came up positive. I could really use someone to talk to. Are you free?"

"Well—I guess so," answered Clarissa uncertainly. "You mean now?"

"Well, if you don't mind . . ."

"Come on over then."

As Jennifer planted herself behind the wheel of her battered green Chevy, she felt a twinge of excitement at the prospect of rekindling an old friendship. She had not had many girlfriends since leaving high school. Her only contacts had been at work—and now she wasn't working.

She remembered when she had first met Clarissa—at Janice Hogan's party. The Hogans' spacious ranch-style house was crawling with kids from Morrow. The Hogans, especially Janice, were unsnobbish about their wealth. She introduced Jennifer around and finally left her with Clarissa and two of her friends. The two others headed for the pool, leaving Jennifer and Clarissa alone.

"So, Jennifer," Clarissa began, "I hear you come from New Mexico. What do you think of your new home?"

"Well," Jennifer replied, "it's a lot wetter here. I came from the desert part of the state, so I'm not used to all this rain. But I think I'll like it. My dad's into computer hardware, and a lot of it's being made here, so it's ideal for him."

"What are your plans? You going to college?"

"Plans?" she laughed. "Who's got time for plans? Right now, I just want to have a good time."

This attempt to lighten the conversation was lost on Clarissa. Their exchange seemed to wither from that point forward.

The memory of that and other events where they had been together began to surface as she guided her rattling heap down the road. In reviewing them, she came to the painful awareness that each time she had entered into a conversation with Clarissa, it had soon dried up. While they shared friends, they shared no interests—no common ground.

Maybe this won't be the rekindling of a friendship after all, she thought. But it occurred to her that this was the closest thing to someone to share her confusion she was liable to find.

Jennifer had hardly entered Clarissa's house before launching into her story. "The problem is Brad. I've been living with him for about a year—you remember—I told you I went to Acapulco. Anyway, I really think Brad'll marry me, but I'm not sure if the kid would be a plus or a minus. I know he'll probably bring up that we can't afford it yet, but the guy makes good money—I dunno."

Clarissa broke in, "How do you feel about having a baby?"

"I dunno. I guess I never gave it much thought," Jennifer replied. "I suppose if it helped to get us hitched, that might be good. But it could really interfere with our lives. I like babies, but when you want to have a good time, they're so . . . well, I'm just not sure if we're ready for kids yet."

The last phrase lashed out at at Clarissa. She knew that Jennifer's "not ready" meant "inconvenient." She sat silently dueling with the implications. *No!* she thought. *My reasons are not the same as hers. What she means is that it will spoil her good times. With me—us—it will spoil responsible planning.*

Planning for a new car and a bigger house, her conscience added mercilessly.

"I don't think you should use pregnancy as a lever to get Brad to marry you," Clarissa stated. "I take it you haven't told him yet?"

"Naw!" Jennifer said, "I heard that Greenbriar has free counseling, so I went last Saturday but, man, you should'a seen all the picketers. One of the people tried to grab me, so I took off. Yesterday I called one'a those places on the billboard, you know—Pregnant? Need help? Call such and such a number—but I wasn't sure what to say, so I hung up. That's when I decided to call you. By the way, did you get your test in?"

Clarissa was not prepared to discuss her pregnancy with Jennifer, but there was no way to avoid the question. "It was positive," she answered and closed the subject with, "I need to talk with Matthew though, and he's in Washington, DC."

"Movin' in the big leagues, huh?" Jennifer chirped. "Well, at least you guys are married. It's one angle you don't have to worry about. Well, maybe I need to talk to Brad—sorta like you waiting to talk to Matthew."

The conversation drifted to other topics, and eventually Jennifer climbed into her faded green Chevy and drove off in a cloud of exhaust. Clarissa stood staring down the street after her. What was the difference between Jennifer's definition of "inconvenient" and her own? Really, it was a matter of what each valued: she valued stability and security; Jennifer valued enjoyment and freedom. Weren't everyone's values supposed to be equally valid? That was what she had always asserted—but the consequences of that belief put both their decisions on an equal footing. This didn't settle well with Clarissa. *All values may be equal,* she thought, *but some are more equal than others.*

*

Jennifer arrived at the white frame house in the east end of town shortly after 9:30. She parked her beast behind the year-old opalescent black Camaro that Brad drove. He always said that his work required him to look successful; he could sell more business computer systems if the clients thought he and his company looked top flight. It seemed to pay off.

Jennifer sat there, dreading to go in. What would Brad's reaction be to fatherhood? Her parents wouldn't be of much help—hadn't been since she was quite young. They believed in giving children "space" to make their own choices, but Jennifer thought ten years old had been too young for all the space she had been given. She remembered going to her mother then about a crush she had on a boy.

"Well, honey, you are a big girl now. You need to make these kinds of decisions for yourself," her mother had said. Later, when she discovered Jennifer's promiscuity, she acted as though Jennifer should have *asked* about "such important things."

"I've always been here to help you," Mother moaned. There was a lot of smoke and fuming, but in the end she did nothing to curb Jennifer. Her father was never told—he would not have wanted to know.

Jennifer pressed open the car door and walked slowly toward the house. It was an older home, but Brad had put a lot of money and time into fixing it up.

"Hi, Jen," he called out when he heard the door open. "Where you been?" He had his feet propped up, watching basketball. The gas fireplace and the eerie glow of the TV provided the only light. "I already got some dinner, but I sure could have used some company."

"I ran into an old friend from high school. We got to talking—you know . . ." she responded.

"Hey, I've got to tell you about the deal I cooked today," he said with his eyes lit up. "It was great. The big new architectural firm that is putting in that new building downtown? I sold them a system that will be built-in from the foundation up. They are going to get all of the three-dimensional drawing systems that keep continuous calibrations on materials needed—and everything. This sale will bring me a whale of a commission. Looks like Acapulco again, little girl."

Jennifer's face lifted momentarily. "That's great," she said somewhat flatly.

Brad's brows knit. "What's wrong, little girl? You don't look too good."

"Nothing. It's just that I need to talk to you about something when you get some time. Okay?"

Brad sighed and rolled his eyes. "Here we go again. Soon as you start talking with those other women, you start getting ideas. 'Let's get married!'" he mocked. "Well, I've got a few things I want to talk to *you* about, like when're you going to get another job?"

It was an old refrain. Jennifer had been working at an assembly plant when they first met. She was impressed because he was well dressed and about seven years older. About six months after she moved in with Brad, the company laid off half their work force—Japanese competition. She really hadn't been in a hurry to find another job and hoped that if she made him happy by playing homemaker, he might want to get married. Marriage to her was like permanently "going steady." He was a good catch; he had left a five-year relationship with a woman his own age for her. It was all very flattering. He worked hard, earned good money, and loved to party on his own time. Jennifer wanted that to go on forever.

"But I've been looking," Jennifer lied, "and there's just not a lot out there."

"Hey, I just don't like you hanging around the house all day. You don't need to become a brain surgeon; any job is better than none," he said as if repeating a formula. "So what did you want to talk about?"

"Never mind," she intoned. It was hopeless. She wearily walked by him, showered, and went to bed.

Before she dropped off to sleep, Brad came into the room. "I'm sorry I got after you that way. Guess I was just worried about your being late. Really, what did you want to talk about?"

"You sure you won't get mad?"

He shook his head.

"Well, I've been real careful with the pill, but I found out I'm pregnant." Seeing him about to react, she plunged on, "I did my part; it's just that the pill isn't 100 percent. There's only one thing that is—and I'm sure you're not ready for that!"

This caught him off guard, and she saw the smirk on his face. "So what's the big deal? You get an abortion—I can pay for that—and everything is the same again, right?"

"I dunno, Brad," Jennifer said. "I'm kind of feeling like I want this baby."

"But it costs about two grand to have a kid, and that doesn't count raising him after he's born. That'd also mean you couldn't work for a while. That's pretty expensive!"

"But you make as much or more than lots of guys with kids—and what about this big sale?"

"I don't know," he replied, rubbing his chin with his hand. "That would mean no more Acapulco—no more ski trips. No, I can't do that now. You're going to have to get rid of it."

Jennifer knew that tone. There was no appeal—for now. She offered no protest; she knew it would simply anger him. That night she lay awake far into the night, wrestling with the quandary. Her child was much like Clarissa's; a little girl about the same age, just now feeling the wash of tension already familiar to Clarissa's daughter.

4 THE SOUND OF STEEL

It was an official-looking envelope that Bud retrieved from the mailbox. He recognized it immediately as another in the steady stream of notices that flowed from the county courthouse to his home in its close-in, older neighborhood. There were always changes of court dates, notices on bench probations, and other details related to the bureaucratic conduct of justice where the worst crime was to cause turmoil in the system.

He sighed, "What now?" as he turned over the enclosure and ripped the envelope along the flap fold. Fishing the document out, he began reading and then stopped. The words *ASSAULT II* jumped off the page. In stark disbelief, he checked the name—ELGIN GRANT TOWER. It was dated as of the last rescue. "They couldn't be . . ." he began, but the thought was amputated by the sound of the phone.

"Hello," he answered.

"'ello, Bud? Bill here. I suppose you got one of these Assault II notices?"

"Yeah, I just now . . ."

But Bud's attorney was already rolling. "This is pure fabrication. I made some calls. They say they have people who'll testify that you shoved this Mz. Whatsername."

"Risner, Joan Risner's her name. How is she?" Bud interjected.

"Risner? How's Risner? Okay, from what I hear, except she's claiming persistent headache, dizziness, neck injury, mental anguish . . . you know, the usual. Anyway, Assault II doesn't depend entirely on damage but on intent to do harm."

There was Bill Wright—thinking like a lawyer. Bud's intent behind the question was to find out Joan's condition, not to check for his own culpability. Bill was a good man. About 25 percent of his practice was devoted to *pro bono* work, primarily for the pro-life rescuers. His rumpled appearance belied his agile, creative legal mind. Beneath the bewildered expression, the short, dumpy frame, and the wrinkled suit lay the soul of an excellent legal fencer. The other major clinic in town, the Gaia Women's Center, had closed under the legal pressure of Bill's suit against both it and the state. Gaia had operated for seven years without state licensing, squeezing through the regulatory language which exempted clinics that did "procedures routinely performed in a physician's office." Wright had argued that late-term abortions, such as the Gaia Women's Center performed, were only rarely done in doctor's offices. The vast majority were done in a hospital. The case taxed the Gaia Women's Center's resources, and it appeared they could lose. They could not hope to comply with health and safety standards if they were forced to be licensed. The final blow came when their insurance company canceled coverage.

"Listen, I don't want you to talk to the press if they call. We'll have a press conference—on our own terms. We'll get this Assault II hogwash cleared up pronto!" Bill said and was gone.

Bud stood still, the phone humming its dial tone in

one hand and the new charge notice in the other hand, for what seemed like hours. He was wondering what Regina would have made of all this.

Those six years of marriage had been wonderful. Everyone had loved Regina's infectious laugh. She was so congenial, so caring, that it surprised people when she would come to a fast boil over crass, cold politicians and bureaucrats with their thick-headed approach to human problems.

Regina and Bud had had no children, not by choice but by physical impossibility; a childhood infection had left her barren. Neither had given up hope; they both believed in miracles. The miracle they prayed for happened, but a midnight collision because of a brake failure stole both of Bud's miracles away. His despair lasted for almost a year. But that was long ago . . .

It still hurt to think of her. Bud had not remarried, at first because he measured everyone by Regina's impossible standard, but later because his time had become so occupied that a social life seemed out of the question.

She would have been involved with this long before I was, he thought as the squawking tone of the still uncradled phone brought him out of his reverie.

✶

Joan Risner relaxed on one of the many-sized pillows that, along with a low table, comprised her living room furniture. The appearance of spontaneity was carefully calculated. Two antique floor lamps standing in opposite corners, like boxers awaiting the sound of the bell, granted light to the room. The bookshelves along the wall were stocked with the classics she loved—*The Iliad* and *The Odyssey, Plato's Republic, Paradise Lost, Shakespeare's*

Collected Works—and the classics she needed—*The Female Eunuch, Against Our Will.*

Joan had inherited the house from her grandmother a couple of years ago along with enough money to put the place in shape. She had wisely made the investment. The two college girls who rented the second bedroom were more friends than boarders; they were among the regulars from the college who came out to Greenbriar clinic as escorts.

She was off from her regular job as a dental assistant after, as the paper put it, "sustaining injuries from a scuffle with a trespassing anti-abortion protester." But it wasn't her injuries that now troubled her as she mulled over the paperwork provided by the Pro-Choice Coalition lawyer, she thought. She knit a brow and brushed back her long, straight, brown hair as she read the outline of the testimony she was to give. *I don't like this*, she thought. The idea of lying about what happened at the clinic was distasteful, but here she was, collecting from Greenbriar's liability insurance for her time off and conspiring to put the troublesome Dr. Tower away for a while.

Joan knew Dr. Jarvis had been in to see his old school chum, District Attorney Van Houten. Van Houten, a devout pro-choice man, was really jazzed; he felt this could scatter the anti-abortion movement in the area. Even the questions and the controversy over Tower's rescues by themselves were threatening the movement. Van Houten had tried to help in the past by assisting in the drafting of an anti-noise ordinance to be enforced around "medical facilities." But even the normally sympathetic ACLU found it offensive to free speech; the unions saw it as a threat against the unionized hospital workers' right to strike. It died before it got to council. Still, it showed where Van Houten's sentiments lay.

The attorney from PCC, Ramsey Briar, had spent over two hours with her this morning taking her through the important details of her testimony. She couldn't help feeling that Van Houten and Briar had discussed this beforehand. This wasn't just perjury; it was complicity with the DA's office—an odd situation for a political leftist like Joan. Briar was also Family Life's attorney. Joan felt a distinct discomfort that seemed to be stirring deeper issues of the heart.

She stretched her slightly stocky frame across the pillows. *Talk about tangled webs*, Joan thought. *But Tower deserves more than a thirty-day slap on the wrist for what he's doing. If the law, as it is, can't deal properly with him, maybe I need to help it along.* Still she felt like a conspirator in an arcane dystopia novel as she buried herself in the paperwork.

*

The *News-Clarion* had reported the altercation at the clinic, but it entirely missed mentioning the thirteen-year-old girl who had exited with Bud Tower. She had gone home that day with a live baby rather than an empty womb. When her mother found out, her anger erupted in a string of obscenities.

"You're a useless whore," she screeched. "The welfare was gonna pay for that abortion, ya know. It's not like ya had to pay for it yourself. I'm not raisin' any more brats, not even yours. I gotta good mind to take you back down there to get that kid taken care of—maybe get you fixed to boot! As a matter of fact—"

Ginger knew what that tone of voice meant. She got up and sped out the door.

"You come back here!"

The slam of the screen door was the only answer. A couple of blocks away, Ginger reached into her purse and pulled out the wadded-up card given to her by the sidewalk-counselor. At the first pay phone, she dropped in her coin and punched up the number. She felt relief as the voice on the other end said, "Crisis Pregnancy Center. May I help you?"

"Yes, I'm Ginger Buck and I've got a big problem."

*

"Yeah, the good Dr. Jarvis has a *vice* grip on city hall," Wright thundered, secretly satisfied by Bud's wince at his pun. "That—that—well, there's no Christian way to say it—that slime got his zoning variation for Greenbriar through council—with the City Manager's inestimable help—packaged in a three-inch bundle of boring budget stuff. He practically has the DA in his back pocket. Fraternity brothers, phaa!"

"So, what's the latest from the DA's office?" Bud inquired.

Bill Wright rubbed his bald spot, heaved a sigh, and said, "Well, I convinced Van Houten that Assault II is ludicrous—I mean, how could he show intent? Now he's come back with Assault III. All he's got to show is that you were reckless—which he can do if his witnesses hold up. Assault III is still felony territory, class C—a five-year max. And Judge Peter Tovelli again—I wish he'd peter out!"

Bud grimaced. "Do you ever run out of those terrible puns?"

"I get a great deal of *sadis*faction from them," Bill replied with a wink. Then, as he left the room, he tossed over his shoulder, "Say, if you're prone to high blood pressure, shouldn't you cut back on *assault*?"

That evening Bud descended the stone steps to the church basement for mid-week Bible study. Immediately, Bill Foxe, the short, heavy-built plumber, accosted him.

"How could you do it?"

"I didn't."

"But the papers—the TV—they said—" Bill plunged ahead, "Well, they said you pushed her. They got witnesses!"

"All I can say is that it isn't true. You actually believe the *News-Clarion*? Now I'm not trying to compare myself, but I seem to recall Paul the apostle and his friends being called all kinds of things—blasphemers, destroyers of temples. What would have happened to the early church if they'd believed everything they heard about other believers? We shouldn't be so quick to believe accusations."

"True," came from the lanky, silver-haired John Radke standing in the far right corner, "but you have to admit that the accusations would never have been possible if you hadn't been inside the clinic—breaking the law. What about Romans 13—submitting to every ordinance of man?"

"Well, Rad, I had to take all that into account when I first decided to do this. I mean, what do you do when the law forbids you to obey an express command of God? What if, for instance, the law said that it was illegal to feed the hungry? Should Salvation Army just fold up and blow away? Should individual Christians stop obeying the command to feed the hungry? The way I read my Bible, if the legitimate government does one of two things—one, requires us to actively sin, as when Shadrach, Meshach, and Abednego were commanded to worship the idol; or, two, forbids us to obey a direct command of God, such as when Peter was told not to preach—then we must disobey the law. Proverbs 24:11-12 tells us to rescue those being taken away to death and warns us against taking refuge in excuses like 'I didn't know it was happening.' Nearly all of the heroes of the Bible disobeyed the law.

"You must remember that what Corrie Ten Boom did in hiding Jews from the Nazis during World War II was no different from what those who are saving babies today are doing. Most of the churches opposed what she did, saying Christians should obey *every* law of man. Don't you see that interpretation of Romans makes current state law, rather than the Bible, the final arbiter of right and wrong?"

"But isn't the real battle for the souls of the girls and even of the abortionist?" asked Janet Simms.

"Sure," chimed in her husband, Rod, "if we prayed for the abortionists and the women and we witnessed to them, they would get saved and not get abortions, or do them."

"That's a good point, Rod," Bud answered, fixing his eyes on both of them, "but let's be consistent. Do we use the same reasoning for other crimes? Take, for instance, theft. Do we just pray for and witness to thieves, or do we also support laws against theft and create police departments to enforce those laws? I seem to recall that your house was burglarized about six months ago. When they caught the guys and you found your things had already been sold, your response was very Christian. But no one suggested for a minute that these men simply be preached to, prayed for, and released."

Then Jim Fisher, the study leader, entered the fray. "Well, then, we should be supporting a human life amendment and other laws to stop or regulate abortion. Just like with theft, a major part of the Christian response is writing and supporting just laws to protect everyone, right? So maybe we should concentrate on the Congress and state legislatures. After all, the ultimate goal is to stop abortion. That's where the battle is."

"I might agree," Bud replied, "if we were only concerned about saving babies ten years from now, but over 4,400 babies died today. Where's our responsibility to those kids? It's like the command to feed the hungry. It's a wonderful idea to set up a plan where no one need ever go hungry after—let's say—next year, but that does not fulfill our Scriptural obligation to feed that hungry person at our doorstep today. Ultimate goals are wonderful as long as they don't stop us from attaining the immediate goal of saving lives. It's the difference between abortion as an issue, and abortion as a real, brutal death of a human being."

No one seemed to notice as the time passed that the study had never officially started. Jim Fisher had long advocated relating Biblical truth to modern problems. He saw no need to bring the meeting to order. He sat back and watched as Bud's simple statements drove most there to thoughtful silence.

Once again John Radke spoke up. "But what alternative do people have? Most people don't know how hideous abortion really is—and the girls, if there is help available, they don't know about it. Maybe the real battle is educating the public."

Bud Tower looked over the group and sighed. He knew that confrontation had its negative results in situations like these. After what seemed an interminable wait, he carefully and graphically described each method of abortion: the hideous result of suction aspiration when a two-inch body is sucked through a quarter-inch tube; the bloody reality of the D&C procedure slicing parts and pieces one at a time from the panicking child; the brutality of the D&E's clamp ripping, crushing, and tearing the tiny body, dragging it from the safety of the womb. He asked the grimacing audience, "How many of you were aware of those details before I recited them?" Slightly over half the hands showed.

"Now, of you that raised your hands, how many are involved in any way in pro-life activities?" The hand of Jim Fisher barely crept above his lapel.

"Herein lies the problem: One and a half million babies a year in this country are killed in spite of all legislative, educational, and Christian efforts. One says that the battle should be to preach the gospel; another says the battlefield is in the courts and legislatures; others say the war is over the minds, and that education is the necessary weapon. Sidewalk counseling and picketing are educational tools—front-line educational efforts. Yet all of these combined failed to save the lives of one and a half million of 'the least of these, my brethren.'

"No, none of these is the battlefield. The womb, what should be the safest place on earth, is the battlefield. That's where the blood is shed. The Church—the whole body of Christ—needs to first repent—then act, or this country will wind up looking like the desolation of Edom in Isaiah 34. You ought to read it over sometime. What happens to a nation that abandons God is not a pretty picture."

There was a long silence. "Let's close in prayer," Jim Fisher whispered.

As Bud bowed his head to pray, he noticed the white head and frail form of Mrs. Roberts in the corner. Her bright blue eyes were fixed on him. Bud always felt tense around her. She looked like his third grade teacher, Miss Bergstrom, and he always imagined she wore the same tight-lipped look of disapproval. Miss Bergstrom had been surprised that year to find, not one, but three black students in her class. She had never had even one before. Her peculiar way of saying "negroes" made one imagine that she was holding some undesirable object at arm's length.

Mrs. Roberts's voice strongly resembled Bergstrom's, and when she looked directly at Bud, it always seemed to be a hard look. Bud was one of just a few blacks in this congregation, and Mrs. Roberts had been there when he became the first black member. His thoughts were just returning to the prayer when the rest of the group muttered "amen" and began to collect purses and Bibles from under the chairs.

Bud did not leave the room until late that night. About a dozen people remained with questions: How can we get more involved? What can we do to help?

Perhaps I'm getting cynical in my old age, Bud thought to himself as he wheeled his late-model Chrysler home through the moonlit night, *but it's my guess that, at most, only one of those people will become involved.* He shook his head. "Naw, I have to believe that there will be more laborers in the field." Still the knot in his stomach grew as he thought of the increasing legal complications and the weakness of the pro-life movement in the area. Even his pastor, once a regular visitor to the picket lines, now seemed always to be busy with "ministry duties."

The phone was ringing when Bud entered the house. He left the key dangling in the open door while he grabbed the receiver.

"Hey, Bud," came the voice of Pastor Jim Hite. "I figured you would be home by now."

"What's up, Jim?"

"Just met a friend of yours today," Hite said brightly. "Her name is Ginger Buck."

"Ginger Buck? Oh, Ginger . . . the girl who came out of the clinic with me last week."

"That's right, Bud," Hite said. "Bill Wright's got her

case. The mother wants her to have an abortion, but she's ready to fight to keep the baby. Wright brought her by for counseling."

"That's great," Bud said. "How did all this happen?"

"It's a long story," Hite replied. "You know I have never approved of your rescues, but this girl walked right past me as I picketed the day you were arrested. My sign didn't save that baby, but your rescue did. Biblically, I *could* find justification for some civil disobedience, and this has really made me think. You know, the girl even seems interested in the gospel."

Bud was grateful for Hite's involvement. It had begun slowly with a yearly picket. He was one of the few pastors involved at all. Most said they were only called to preach. Bud was tempted to ask if they would merely preach to a hungry person at the door, or if they would add the blessing, "Be ye warmed and filled." But Hite was cautiously active—picketing, sidewalk counseling, public speaking.

Bud remembered his cynical thoughts on the drive home. *I guess You're way ahead of me, Lord,* his prayer went heavenward. "That's really good news," he told Hite. "It's just what I needed right now."

*

Ginger Buck's mom "would like to have gone through the roof," as Ginger put it, when Bill Wright called her to let her know that Ginger was safe at his home. "She has retained me as counsel," Bill said officiously, rocking heel to toe. "She claims you intend to force her to have an abortion. It appears you may have violated Ginger's civil rights—her right of choice." He reveled in this twist of the verbal knife but seriously doubted that the woman would even catch the irony.

"That child is mine," Mrs. Buck responded. "I'm in charge of her medical treatment! You can't keep her at your house. That's kidnapping!"

"I'm afraid you're wrong there, Mrs. Buck," Bill responded evenly. "As Ginger's counsel, I've taken the liberty of contacting the juvenile court with her situation, and they have granted me temporary custody, at Ginger's request, I might add, until this matter can be further investigated."

"I'll sue," Mrs. Buck said. "I tell ya, I'll sue!"

"Then," stated Wright, "we shall have our introduction, as they say, in court," and replaced the receiver carefully in the cradle, with Mrs. Buck's angry buzz still coming over the wire.

*

The *News-Clarion* carried the story straight: "Mom Sues to Force Teen's Abortion." It was a four-inch blurb pasted on the lower crease of the twelfth page, section B. There was little sense of the importance of such a case among the *News-Clarion*'s staff, and little sense of irony. If a girl could choose, without parental permission or notification, to have an abortion because of a "right of choice" or a "right of privacy," what became of those rights if she made the choice to have the baby? Bill Wright was fond of telling people that the case was *pregnant* with implications.

The Pro-Choice Coalition was having difficulty with this case. After all, Ginger defied everything they stood for. PCC had always maintained that clinic invasions were terrorism because a woman in the clinic had already made her choice. Ginger's mind had changed while in the clinic. They were all in favor of a woman's choice, but in their hearts they knew there was only one right choice—especially for a poor welfare kid of thirteen.

The Children's Services Department wanted no part of the miry legal ground and left Wright and Mrs. Buck to fight it out, eyeing only the eventual custody of Ginger—and the baby.

Mrs. Buck brought suit against the state and Crisis Pregnancy Center for depriving her of custody and parental rights unlawfully—and a whole ream of other charges. Ramsey Briar agreed to take up the case, *pro bono*. In truth there was a surreptitious pipeline of funds which urged his compassion for the woman's predicament; an irrigation from the generous accounts of Dr. Jarvis and many of Family Life's supporters.

In the preliminary hearing, the plaintiff's argument, simply stated by Briar, was that the elder Ms. Buck had legal custody and prior rights in the health decisions affecting the younger Ms. Buck. "Such parental rights should not be lightly tampered with by the state," Briar concluded.

"Your Honor," Wright opened, "it is not needful for me to inform the bench of the U. S. Supreme Court ruling of *Roe v. Wade* giving pregnant women privacy in their choice of medical treatment. This right has been maintained by other courts for women of my client's age. I do not think that it is the desire of this court to *wade* in seas where the Supreme Court found it difficult to *row*." Judge Callivan looked narrowly at Wright and, under cover of judicial decorum, said nothing. An almost imperceptible smirk told Wright that he had not exceeded his limits, so he added, "I believe that *Roe v. Wade* gives the woman the right to *either* choice."

"Recess until 2," Callivan said, rising quickly and retreating to his chambers.

"All rise!" the bailiff cried almost too late.

*

Judge Callivan reentered the maple-paneled court-room at 2:32 P.M. sharp and, brushing aside the formalities, announced that the suit was "groundless" and dismissed it. Bill Wright secretly chuckled. His only discomfort came from what this case might portend for parental rights. Briar vowed to carry the issue to district court.

5 SKIRMISHES ON THE HOME FRONT

She didn't know that her father was returning from his trip, but she felt a buzz of cautious excitement. In the midst of the ambiguity, there lay a carpet of tension. She had grown accustomed to the feeling. Absently, she gummed her knuckle and snuggled down for a nap. Her free-floating world spun as she drifted from side to side, tumbling loosely in the warm, wet cavern.

*

Matthew was late. He was late in more ways than one. The gaggle of negotiations with the Pentagon cost him two more days in Washington than he had anticipated. The military negotiators had minds like steel boxes—no way in and no way out. Now it was 1:30 A.M. on the airport tarmac, the plane having disgorged its living contents in confusion onto the black, rain-slicked surface. He couldn't remember the last time he had met a plane or flown in one that had arrived on time. He noted with wry humor that the monitors in airports had columns for both the scheduled and the actual arrivals. Things were even more bizarre at smaller airports such as this, where a long-standing tradition of practiced inefficiency was compounded by the low pay and cliff-hanging finances.

He stopped in the lobby to adjust the shoulder strap for his gray nylon carry-on and reengaged his hand on the morocco leather briefcase his father had given him for his last birthday. The shuttle to downtown awaited, its diesel engine chugging to keep the inadequate heater alive. Matthew heaved his large frame aboard, deposited his luggage on the rack, and turned to present his ticket to the weary driver. Home was on the edge of town opposite the airport, so it was a simple economic decision to opt for a shuttle downtown before resorting to the more expensive taxi to take him home. Casco, in the end, would pay the bill, but there was no sense in taking a taxi for the full journey.

The shuttle left the terminal with only two other passengers aboard. Matthew stared out the tinted window and, with some effort to ignore the reflected interior light, stared at the spangles of light glistening from the city center. The rain on the windows only enhanced that glittering look.

Yawning, he turned to see the dreary interior of the vehicle. The fluorescent light cast a greenish pall over the other occupants; in an eerie way it reminded him of some kind of bus for the undead. He could see by his reflection in the safety glass that he looked no better. It brought a smirk and a sniff, a tired substitute for a chuckle, as he thought of the low grade movie someone might make— *Bus of the Undead* or *Shuttle Zombies*. The loneliness of the scene only sharpened his yearning to be home.

A forty-five-minute ride in the zombie express deposited him outside the Downtowner Hotel. It was nearly another half hour by taxi to home. The only appealing thing about the prospect was the word *home*.

The taxi driver was nothing like the shuttle's man. The cabbie hooked his captive audience into a long tale, and by some strange ability was able to give expression through the back of his head. By the time Matthew opened the door of the hack before his home, he had become an expert on the life and family of Dennis Martin.

At 3:15 A.M., he was finally there. Carefully, Matthew turned the key and cracked open the door. He booted himself mentally as he was brought to teeth-gnashing awareness of the unoiled hinge. By the silhouetted lump on the divan, it appeared that Clarissa had tried to wait up for him. "I probably won't be in until 2 or 3 in the morning," he had said to her on the phone.

She had replied, "No harm in my trying, is there?"

He closed the door as carefully as he could and looked at her sleeping form. He shook his head and grinned as he thought about the "career-minded, independent woman" he had married, waiting up for him until all hours. He was pleased that her drive and ambition had not driven out their love for one another.

Matthew crept to the bathroom, cleaned up a little, and stowed his bag in the bedroom closet. He shook Clarissa awake and, clasping her slender shoulders, led her stumbling off to bed. "Good night," he said as he pecked her forehead and left her to slumber on.

*

Her sleep went almost uninterrupted. Only once that night did she awake with a start and a flurry, but it was only a dream. Soon she slumbered again, reigning in her private universe.

*

The sun rose brilliantly the next morning, glittering on the still-wet streets, grass, and bushes. "Clarissa," Matthew called as the familiar creak of the front door signaled her return from her morning run, "I've got to put in a lot of overtime this week to catch up on the work I missed while in Washington. I'll probably be in late all week."

"Oh, no," Clarissa frowned, "I really need some time with you. Couldn't you delegate some of the work?"

"'Fraid not, Hon," Matthew replied. "I could use some time with you too, but you know how it is."

Matthew had been thinking of time together in its romantic sense, but Clarissa was still deep in her private struggle. She needed someone to affirm her decision, yet she refused to acknowledge it. She said no more.

The next week dragged interminably through its required seven increments, Matthew's late-night arrivals unnoticed by his sleeping wife. She only saw him stretched across the bed in the morning as she tugged on her blue and gold running shoes and hastily retreated through the door. Then he was straightening his tie when she returned from yet another sweaty run. Matthew continued his work through the weekend, not that it would have made a difference in their togetherness. Clarissa attended a long-awaited business seminar both days.

*

She was one week over the mark. She had crossed the imaginary threshold of the second trimester, and her heart was not one whit different for its passing. Beating stronger than ever, it fed her one-ounce body with nutrients and oxygen. What difference there was between her first and second trimester states was a matter of speculation by courts of law; she only continued to grow as she always had.

A new sensation invaded her consciousness—the salty taste of the amniotic fluid. She grimaced as she swallowed a mouthful, but soon she didn't notice.

*

"Mayline. Clare speaking. May I help you?"

"Yeah, you can help me eat a couple of steaks tonight. When can I pick you up?"

"Well, I don't know. My husband might object—"

"Don't worry about it. He's always too busy flying to Washington or burning the cathode tubes out of his computer at Casco. What d'ya say? How about 6:00?"

"Well, only if you're discreet," Clarissa laughed. She would finally be able to talk to Matthew alone.

Later, seated at the table, she chased the Caesar salad around the plate with her fork while Matthew relished his New York steak and baked potato. "You're not eating much," he observed.

"I suppose I'm just preoccupied," she replied. "I've been needing to talk to you since the day you left for Washington, but the phone just wasn't the right place, and—well, you know what the last week's been like."

"Yeah, I know. And I'm sorry, Hon, but—"

"No, I'm not upset about that, but I have an important decision to make, and I want to make it together with you."

"Well? Shoot."

Clarissa sighed inwardly, firming her resolve. "You know how carefully we've planned things. Well, we have a little unexpected deviation. I found out the day you left that I'm pregnant—I'm over thirteen weeks right now."

Matthew's fork, complete with its piece of steak perched on the end, halted before his open mouth. Slowly the fork lowered and was abandoned on the plate. Matthew straightened his shoulders and leaned back against the plush red velvet chair. She could almost hear him mentally trying to fit this ungainly new fact into their plans. Right now, Clarissa knew a baby would never fit, but she knew that Matthew would have to first satisfy himself of that.

Silent eons passed before Matthew said, "That's great! It's a little different than the original plan, but—I think we can work it out."

Clarissa was speechless, but only momentarily. "Work it out? What about our plans? What about providing our own home and all that for our children? What about my job?"

"Take it easy," Matthew said, trying to soothe her. "Take it easy. All the details can be worked out later. I mean, what do you want to do—get an abortion? It's not like you're some unwed teenager. What's the purpose in being married if we can't raise a family?"

"Well, I'll tell you this much. I have no intention of discussing this paternal chauvinism of yours in a public place, so when you're ready to leave, I'll see you out in the car." She rose quickly and strode through the elaborately carved front door. Other diners hardly seemed to notice.

Matthew paid the bill and followed.

They rode home in silence. Matthew squirmed behind the wheel as he mentally tried to mount an argument for his position. *What did I say that was so chauvinistic?* he wondered as they pulled into the drive. He opened the garage and locked the car inside as Clarissa disappeared into the house.

"Do you actually think that only unwed mothers

need abortions?" he heard as he entered the living room. "The whole abortion issue is over whether women can *control* their own fertility, whether couples can control their own fertility—so that women or couples won't be at the mercy of biology when they plan their lives. So people won't be impoverished by having children when they are not convenient." She winced inwardly as she heard that word come out of her own mouth, but she quickly hardened and continued, "Abortion isn't just so some sexually hyperactive teen won't have to be embarrassed, it is so responsible people whose birth control fails, like ours did, won't have to abandon their plans for better lives and careers."

Matthew hesitated, trying to call together, as if by magic, an argument. "I'm sorry, Hon," he said haltingly. "I just don't see what the big deal is in our case. It's not like we're going to go broke or anything. Most of our plans will just take a little longer, that's all. I always thought abortions were for serious problems, not just convenience."

That last word was like a stick stirring up a shower of sparks from the smouldering embers in her conscience. "Convenience?" she cried. "You think *my career* is a mere convenience?"

"That's not what I meant—" he said as she solidly closed the bedroom door on him.

"Maybe you need to think this over, Matthew," she said coolly through the closed door. "I wanted this to be a partnership decision, but it seems you have your mind made up. Maybe we need to spend some time apart to think this through. I'm going to Aunt Jeanne's place for a while."

"But—" he burbled.

"It's not that far away. She'll put me up, and we can both cool off."

Matthew felt she was cool enough already, but he said nothing as he watched her drive off in the older import. *It needs a tune-up.* He wondered if the incongruous thought related only to the car.

*

Clarissa wound her way up the gravel drive that led to the back of the ten-acre wooded lot. The Douglas fir and vine maple filtered moonlight down to the rutted path before her. She knew she would not be taking Aunt Jeanne entirely by surprise. The inconspicuous electric eye at the head of the drive had telegraphed the warning ahead. This was not a simple country cottage, for all its rustic appearance. Only careful grooming maintained the illusion of being "out in the boonies." Actually, downtown was a mere forty minutes away by clogged freeway.

Clarissa's parents were a good deal closer, but she felt distinctly uncomfortable about revealing her predicament to them. Not that they would oppose her, but she had never been close to her mother. And her father—well, they had been friends, but this subject Clarissa felt would stretch his comfort zone to the breaking point. Besides, both of them were probably too busy to bother with her first marriage squabble. Dad was likely to be out of town, as he often was since he had moved up to a management position, and Mom, though present, always seemed distant.

Aunt Jeanne had little to do with her time and money other than cultivate the image of a country cottage. She was not truly eccentric, only a little different. Her last husband had left her well-off, but she had attained a measure of success on her own writing nonfiction, mostly of a political and philosophical nature.

As Clarissa's headlights swung round to the front porch of the rambling home, they clearly illuminated the spare figure of a forty-five-year-old woman dressed in a loose-fitting muslin peasant blouse and a mid-calf length Madras print skirt. She appeared to casually lean against the door frame, half in and half out of the house. Clarissa knew that was a ruse. Serious crimes plagued this countrified-swank area. The electric eye had done more than announce company. It had switched on the porch light and the brilliant quartz-halogen lamp that flooded the parking area. Jeanne's hand rested on a 9mm Beretta stowed in a bookshelf near the door.

Jeanne's eclectic interests encompassed strong liberal stands on most issues, contrasted with opposition to gun control and support of capital punishment. She was a dead shot with her weapons and her words.

Clarissa set the parking brake, flung open the door, and planted her feet on the pebbled surface of the drive. She put her hands in the air crying, "Don't shoot! I come in peace!"

Recognition crossed Jeanne's face. "Come on in," she said, "but be quick about it. I don't want to heat this porch any longer."

Clarissa snatched her bag and dragged it into the well-lighted sunken living room. Sinfully comfortable couches and chairs were scattered through the room to form separate enclaves for conversations. She hadn't seen her aunt since she showed up at the wedding with her disapproving look. "Marriage for a young girl like you is ridiculous," she had said boldly. "There are so many great things of life to sample when you're young. You can get married any time."

After Clarissa dropped her bag, Jeanne embraced her.

Then holding her at arm's length, she said knowingly, "What's wrong?" Jeanne was noted for her inquisitions.

"Well, it's Matt. You see . . ."

＊

Matthew piloted his small Buick through the morning traffic several days after Clarissa's abrupt departure. They had spoken on the phone last night. She had rebuffed his two earlier attempts to call with a "Give it a couple of days." He reviewed the conversation. All of the "should-have-saids" heaped upon his now-agile mind, though they had deserted him the night before. He lacked the subtlety and tact required for these oral tussles.

The "Wa-a-ah!" of the horn from a passing car woke him to the realization that he was halfway across the center dividing line. He angrily whipped the wheel, overcompensating and nearly sideswiping a blue Mercedes in the right lane. "Wouldn't my insurance company love to see that bill?" he muttered to himself as he grinned sheepishly and shrugged at the driver of the expensive chariot. The driver returned a universal signal of derision. "I'd better pay attention to my driving." But it was too late. The flash of red and blue appeared in his rearview mirror. He could feel its pointed finger of shame directed at him. Finding an opening in traffic, he delivered the Buick to the curb and fished out his license. Matthew rolled his eyes heavenward and thought, *My first ticket, oh, boy!*

He rolled his window down in time to hear, "Drivin's a little erratic, wouldn't't'cha say?" in a slow drawl.

All he could see was the citation book and pen held near the polished belt buckle, but Matthew knew the voice.

"C'd I see'er license, ser?" came the drawl again.

"Jim?" Matthew queried as he handed over the laminated rectangle.

Looking up at the officer's sunglasses, Matthew was not deceived by the cover. "Jim! Jim Davis? Right?"

"Matthew," Jim said, finally recognizing him, "Hey, boy! What'r you up to? Oh, I know. Workin', eatin', and sleepin', right?"

Matthew nodded wondering where his old companion had developed the Southern drawl.

"Hey, what'dya say I call this a warnin'," Jim said. "We can't stand round here all day yammerin'—got a quota to meet. How's about getting together after work at Stanley's—*you* remember Stanley's—I get off at 4:30. You're not busy tonight, are ya?"

Matthew shook his head. "I'm free. I can meet you about quarter after five. That sound okay?"

"Sure," Jim said handing back the license. "See ya then."

*

Matthew's daughter swam around delighted. She barely noticed the constant leakage of tension into her world any longer. It seemed to be a constant and persistent level of tightness. It was tolerable. Just as born children often adjust to bizarre family situations, so she too had come to accept as normal this taut sensation.

*

Matthew dove into the smoke-filled interior of Stanley's burger joint and coughed. In high school he and Jim had been habitués of the greasy dive, but he didn't remember it being so hazy. In the corner of the red and white interior, next to the raucous jukebox, a hand signaled him over. Matthew squeezed past the intervening tables and guided his bulky body into the narrow bench of the booth.

"Buy y'a beer, Matthew?" Jim offered.

The reminiscence began in earnest as the waitress delivered the pitcher, and they both leaned forward toward the center of the table to overcome the competition of the music machine. They sat for an hour and a half. The crowd thinned, and the music grew milder with spaces of silence between.

"Well, I c'n guess what'chr up to now," Jim said. "Still workin' for yer ol' man, right? I hardly ever saw you after ya turned sixteen 'cause you were always workin'."

"Yeah," Matthew replied. "He kept me pretty busy. I went on to get an associate degree in business. I needed it to move up in the company. I got married about six months ago—"

"Hey, that's great!"

"I tried to find you to send an invitation, but I couldn't," Matthew said apologetically.

"S'okay," Jim replied. "I've been purty scarce. M' folks moved to Florida."

"Well, I've been getting real involved at Casco. I figure that by the time my dad retires, I can expand the company to at least four factories in different parts of the country. By the time I retire—"

"Whoa, there, boy!" Jim reared back. "You really plan stuff, don'cha? Got yer burial plots bought yet?"

"As a matter of fact . . ." Matthew smiled. "Jim, I heard you were married."

"Yeah. A gal I met while I took po-lice science after high school. We were livin' together fer a while, ya know.

Well, she got pregnant an' I'm not one to shirk my responsibilities so . . ."

Matthew cringed inwardly. Jim had always been the macho man, even long after that sort of thing had gone out of fashion. Jim was an example of chivalry—or chauvinism—above and beyond the call of culture. *Is that the way I sound to Clarissa?* he wondered. But Matthew felt uncomfortable about revealing the current sticky status of his marriage, so he focused the conversation on Jim.

"What about your kid?" Matthew asked.

"Oh, Jimmy? Yeah, he's a good kid. Can't play ball worth beans though," he said with a grin. "He's only a half a year old. Y' throw him a ball, an' he jus' sits there an' drools."

"You haven't told me much about your wife either," Matthew prodded.

"Rachel. Her name's Rachel. Like I said, I met her while I was in school. She was takin' some business classes—y'know, secretary stuff. Anyway, I tried to line her up with a secretary job in the department, but she said she didn't wanna work in a cop shop. She really wants to start a business of her own, and we're schemin' on how t' do that. Wants to open a beauty supply store."

"What about Jimmy?" Matthew queried.

"Well, we had a hassle over that f'r a while, but we figger by the time we get this started, the kid'll be old enough f'r day care."

"What about police work? How do you like it?" Matthew asked changing the subject again.

"What? Ketchin' bad-guys? Pretty good, most'a the time. Pretty demanding. Busts up a lot of cop marriages, ya know. Traffic is a bore, but there are some exciting days. Hey, I gotta tell ya about Mac. He was my first partner—

broke me in—and he was one'a my instructors in the police academy.

"When I first went out with Mac, he tol' me how t' handle a rabbit—a guy tryin' t' run away. I as'ed if I should fire a warnin' shot—'at shows how green *I* was—and he said no. He says to jus' grab my riot gun, crack on the pump action, an' yell, 'Run, you dirty, son uf'a . . .'" Jim laughed at the memory. "He tol' me the guy'd be back huggin' my boots in seconds."

For the next half hour, Jim regaled Matthew with the wild adventures of the veteran cop from Georgia. The near-worshipful tones in which Jim spoke about the famous Mac caught Matthew's attention. *So that's the origin of the Southern drawl,* he thought. Someone had once told Matthew that there were only two types of cops—the would-be psychologists and the John Waynes. Here was a John Wayne—in the flesh.

"I hear police work can really be frustrating at times," Matthew commented. "People you work hard to arrest get turned loose in minutes, and courts hand down stingy penalties due to lack of jail space. I read in the *News-Clarion* about the judge threatening to charge the county sheriff with contempt if he exceeded the maximum prisoner allowance. The sheriff ended up releasing over a hundred prisoners, some violent, and it was all televised. And they say that even people arrested for operating drug labs often are only cited and then have to be released."

Jim's face soured. "Yeah, that's true, but the thing that bothers me most are these abortion protesters."

"Abortion protesters? I'd have thought—"

"Yeah! Abortion protesters. Wha'da waste'a my time, draggin' these bums out of the clinic. Why, jest a coupl'a weeks ago—well, I can't figure it. I mean, abortion isn't a good thing but, heck, it's legal. I wouldn't want my wife t' have one, but that ain't th' point. In fact, my ol' lady wanted one—figured we could'n afford the baby, but I talked 'er out of it.

"Anyway, they got this doctor over there—Dr. Tower—you know, that black psychologist—anyway he gets 'em all fired up, and they get to goin' in the place stirrin' up a bunch'a already nervous women. Ticks me off!" Matthew saw an uncharacteristic anger in his friend's eyes as Jim continued, "Arrested this guy four times already—that's only the ones I've been in on. The last time he knocked over some gal that works there. She smacked 'er head on a table and got a pretty bad concussion. Now Tower's charged with assault. Ma'be that'll slow th' bums down—I dunno."

Matthew was taken aback by Jim's vehemence. "You think this Tower guy will get any time—I mean, him being a doctor?" Matthew asked. "Even real criminals don't serve actual prison time anymore."

"Well, 'at's hard to figure," Jim replied rubbing the stubble on his lantern jaw. "The judges have been maxing out the sentences on these people—teach 'em a lesson, ya know, but it hasn't stopped 'em. 'Course trespass only costs thirty days max, but a heavy sentence on this assault beef's liable t' make 'im think twice."

"I guess I didn't think things were that rough over there. I've heard of clinic bombings in other parts of the country and those bomb threats last year, but I guess I never thought about how violent some of those anti-abortion protesters can be," Matthew said.

"Yeah," Jim replied, "we get complaints all'a time from the clinic—harassment, shovin'—stuff like that. Federal boys are looking into the bomb threats. We know who's doin' it—just need more proof."

Taking note of the time, Jim brushed back his straight

blond hair with his hands, stretched out his arms, and said, "Well, gotta go. Wife will wonder where I am. You know, the married life."

Yeah, married life, Matthew thought sourly.

*

Clarissa stretched out on the heavy, wine-colored velvet sofa in her aunt's living room and yawned. It was Saturday—no work, no traffic. The call from Matthew the other night had been so exasperating that she had just told him not to bother calling until he had something new to say. "I haven't had a lazy day like this in ages," she said, looking through the portal into the vast tiled kitchen hung with copper pots and pans. Jeanne was whipping up a souffle.

"I warned you about marriage," Jeanne said with a grin. "You need to dump the bum and go exploring."

Clarissa knew that there was a serious undercurrent to her aunt's jibe, but she would not allow herself to drift in its direction.

"I think that Matthew just needs a little education, that's all," she said, stretching her neck to see the older woman.

Jeanne called back, "Education, my tush! If I were you, and I'm glad I'm not, I'd just go to Greenbriar and do the abortion and tell Matthew to find another baby machine!"

Clarissa knew Aunt Jeanne would do exactly that. "I'll give him some more time. I want him to make this decision *with* me."

"Come on, Clare," Jeanne retorted from the kitchen doorway, hands on her hips and a look of disapproval on her face. "Call it what it is. You've already decided. It's a personal decision for the convenience of your own career. You just want him to affirm your decision. Why bother? That's what the fight for women's rights was all about—so some man's permission isn't necessary for a woman to decide what's good for her own life."

Clarissa was silent.

∗

Her hearing had yet to develop, but she reacted to the water-borne sound vibrations. She felt with interest the blurps and gurgles of her mother's digestive system, the constant whoosh of the lungs, and the thrum-thum, thrum-thum of her mother's heart. She was almost the size of that heart herself.

∗

"Clarissa?"

"Matthew. How are you?"

"Can we talk? I mean—"

"Depends."

"Well, I've been thinking it over and you're right. I just didn't understand the pressure you were under over this decision." There was silence from the receiver, and Matthew continued, "I was talking to Jim Davis the other day—my old friend from school, you remember. He's a cop now, and he was telling me about all the hassles religious fanatics put women through to get an abortion—even when they need it desperately. Well, I guess I didn't understand what pressures you were under; I guess I was just being overbearing by wanting a baby now. Maybe it was just male ego or something."

Matthew waited. The small noises on the other end were without comfort; he could almost hear her thinking.

"Well," she said and paused again. "Well, I just wanted you to understand my position so we could make this decision together."

"Whatever decision you make, I'll be with you," Matthew said confidently. "I want you to do what's best for you. Nobody's got a right to interfere with such a personal decision. I'll even go down to Greenbriar with you."

"I'll see you this evening, Matthew."

Clarissa didn't wait. She punched the number of Greenbriar clinic and set the time. *The Saturday after next— almost two weeks away,* she thought.

"We'll need to do a urine test," the voice intoned.

"But I've had one—at Family Life," retorted Clarissa.

"We have to do one ourselves," the voice returned. "You say you've been to Family Life?"

"Yes. They referred me to you."

"So, you've had counseling?"

"Counseling?"

"Someone at Family Life talked with you about the abortion?"

"Well, a woman there talked with me—"

"Fine then. When was your last period?"

"Fourteen weeks ago."

"Well, that will require a D&E, a second trimester procedure," the nasal voice continued. "We'll need to have you in on Friday morning for the laminaria—we can do the urine then."

"What's that?"

"Oh—the laminaria? It's a thin piece of dried sea-weed—about three inches long and an eighth-inch in diameter. It's placed in the cervix, and overnight it swells, gently opening the neck of the uterus so that the instruments will fit in during the procedure. Actually, the laminaria is part of the procedure. Once it starts to swell, the procedure is irreversible.

"Now, when you come, there may be some picketers outside. There are usually only a few on Friday. You shouldn't have much trouble with them. Just ignore them; they get paid by the hour to harass patients. On Saturday I'd recommend that you come accompanied by a strong supporter. There are usually many more fanatics out then. We'll have escorts to meet you, but it's always nice to have another friendly face. Besides, you will probably feel a bit cramped after the procedure, and maybe someone else should drive. But remember what I said about the laminaria because the anti-choicers tell women that it can be removed. But when they've tried, women have had serious complications. They usually lose the child anyway. Some women have lost their lives. So don't listen to them."

Clarissa listened carefully, absorbing the counsel. After she hung up, she began to pack. Aunt Jeanne appeared in the doorway.

"Planning to run away?"

"Oh, hi, Aunt Jeanne," Clarissa said as she turned her head from the bag before her. "Yeah, I got things straightened out with Matthew—and I made an appointment at Greenbriar."

"Well, I suppose I can't talk you into leaving the bum," Jeanne remarked offhandedly. "But would you like someone to go to the clinic with you?"

"That's the best part, Aunt Jeanne. Matthew offered to come with me."

∗

Here she was, the whole world lined up against her—the lax laws, the cowardly courts, the politic police, the pragmatic politicians, the deceptive doctors, the milquetoast medical associations, the whining women's groups, the strategic social agencies, the small-minded schools, the petty people, the venial voters, the nescient news media, the show business shills, the conspiratorial columnists, and the vacuous voices of the majority—each sharpening its peculiar weapon against the innocent, unwitting victim. But no opponent in the list was as surprising as her father; none so deadly as her mother.

She did not know any of this. Had she known, how would she cry out for help? What voiceless plea would bring for her a champion to her aid?

*

Everywhere she went, she saw babies. Babies! Babies! Babies! Jennifer couldn't resist poking, petting, cooing, and caressing. She hadn't noticed them before. Was it this secret yearning, this growing maternal drive, that kept her hoping against hope to change Brad's mind? She hadn't dared to broach the subject since that first time. She avoided thinking about her daughter playing, bouncing off the walls of the womb within. She could almost feel the baby's soft, warm weight in her arms.

So it startled Jennifer when Brad walked in and asked flatly, "You take care of that kid yet?"

"Well-l-l, I was gonna talk to you about that."

Brad leveled his gray eyes at her, "I told you no and I meant it. I haven't got time or money for this kid. Neither do you. I'll pay for the abortion—whatever it costs—but if you want the kid, you want it on your own."

Jennifer studied the carpet for a moment and then went to her room and cried for an hour.

"Greenbriar Surgicenter," said the nasal voice on the line.

"Yeah, I need to make an appointment."

The rest of the conversation took place as though pre-recorded.

6 A BATTLE AT THE BORDER

Bud's black face beamed as he approached the huddled knot of picketers. "All right, groupies, are we having tea or picketing?" he gently chided.

The knot loosened and stretched into a more purposeful circulating line. Bud fanned through his literature, assuring himself that he was ready.

Just then Dan Munson sauntered up with his picket sign blaring its fluorescent orange and white message, DR. JARVIS KILLS BABIES! Dan wore his hair over his ears, and it tended to twist and turn in the oddest directions. Working a swing shift allowed him to picket at times when others were unwilling or unable to do so. "That creep, Jarvis, drove up a few minutes ago," he said. "He must have been bored again because he has just bought a new classic car."

Bud nodded. "You know, Dan, that sign of yours may be quite effective. Doctors and nurses who used to do abortions have told us that it was their own names publicly displayed as abortionists that pricked their consciences. Picketing their homes also helps—it lets their neighbors know what they do for a living. But calling them names is not very effective. Besides it's a bad attitude—a forbidden attitude for Christians. We're supposed to love our enemies. If that command doesn't apply here, where does it?"

"I suppose you're right, " Dan replied putting his sign down and leaning on it. "But that guy—some of the stuff he says when he's on TV—some of the stuff he says about us—well, I find it hard to love a guy like that."

"Nobody said loving your enemy would be easy," Bud reminded. "But you never know what is going on under the surface with guys like Dr. Piper—or even hard cases like Jarvis."

"It can't be much better than what goes on under the surface of a septic tank," Dan added.

"I've got to admit that a lot of them—especially the doctors—are in this purely for money. There's lots to be made in this bloody trade—short hours and long green. In my practice, I've counseled with several former abortionists. One was from Los Angeles—he'd done over 10,000 abortions. He told me that several times he went out during lunch hour just to relieve the boredom and bought a new car—cash. He used to fly to San Francisco several evenings a week for dinner. But he had many of the symptoms of postabortion trauma, especially the dreams, and the symptoms finally drove him out of the business. The stories of the nurses are worse; they are the ones who have to 'reassemble' the baby to make sure all the parts are there. A lot of them are really suffering, but from the facade they put up, there's no way to tell.

"Take Dr. Piper . . . "

"Please!"

Bud smirked and went on, "Really, Piper has a genuine concern for women. That's why he chose to get into the work he's doing. Did you know that he and a couple others rented the house next to mine after his residency?"

"Well, no . . . "

"That's right. And during that time we had a lot of heavy conversations—this is right when he began doing a lot of abortions at the hospital. Piper is deeply troubled by the violence and brutality of abortion—it bothers him tremendously—but he is convinced that it is in the best interests of women to provide abortion. He's *not* in it for the money, but he's had to harden himself. Some of that comes out as caustic remarks. I wouldn't be surprised if he either quits or goes for psychiatric treatment in a couple of years."

Just then a baby stroller caught Bud's heel from behind. Before he could turn around, two squealing children ran between the two men. "Sorry," the woman with the stroller said.

"It's okay," Bud replied smiling. "One of the hazards of pro-life picketing."

The woman pushed her stroller on, circulating with the protesters.

"When's the trial on the last rescue . . . the one with the assault charge?" The voice came from a drizzle-soaked Martha Foreman. This mother of three somehow managed to find time to put in four hours a week sidewalk counseling. And it was a good thing. She was the most successful counselor in the area. So deft was her technique that there were rumors that the clinic's lawyers were looking into the feasibility of a suit for restraint of trade, possibly including her in a Racketeer Influenced and Corrupt Organizations or RICO suit.

Bud replied, "Monday we start. Talk about getting a speedy trial." He glanced toward the clinic door. "How many have gone in so far?"

"Eight," she said with a grimace. "I called in again last week. Greenbriar is still feeding them the old line about us being paid fanatics seeking to painfully and dangerously rip the laminaria from their bodies. 'Some women even die!'" she imitated the nasal tone of the woman who answered Greenbriar's phone. The pro-lifers had started calling her Rosebud; some had speculated that she was really a machine.

"Get a job!" intruded the voice of a motorist swooshing past on the rain-soaked street. Bud smiled and waved.

"It's their most effective lie. How can they be expected to give it up? You can see the fear in these girls' faces when they come in after being warned about us. You can smell it."

Both their heads went up as they heard a car door slam—Ka-chunk! Up the street was a young woman with a small bag—a dead giveaway. Both men headed for her. From the corner of his eye, Bud noted the vulturelike descent of the escorts. It was a race and the prize was Life. First arrival was not the goal, as the clinic's escorts were allowed to take the victim's mother by the arms. Counselors would try to hand her literature, which the escorts would as quickly tear from her grasp. The counselors could only hope that their pleading voices found the part of the woman's heart that said, "Mother." Sometimes they did.

*

Bud stood tall in his three-piece charcoal-gray wool suit, the gold watch chain casually and inconspicuously draped across the front of the vest. The starched, white collar contrasted with the dark ebony of his skin. His head was covered with a short crop of graying wool.

"Looking sharp, as usual, Dr. Tower." Bill Wright nodded his approval.

"For all the good it'll do," replied Bud.

"Pessimist?" Bill quizzed.

"Realist."

They clattered their way down the early morning emptiness of the county courthouse's dimly-lit corridors to the room marked 322. The bailiff was just unlocking the old wooden doors when they arrived. Waiting as the key rattled in the lock, Bill asked, "Did you hear the latest on Ginger Buck's case? None of the judges are allowing the suit. You saved another baby, Bud.

"The only bad thing is this 'family counseling' they've forced her into. Court ordered it. Nothing but pro-abort propaganda from *that* counselor, but Ginger's hanging tough. I'm going to have her testify for you."

Bud nodded.

They entered the room, and Bill began to arrange his material on the defense table. "I don't think Tovelli's going to allow Choice of Evils as a defense."

"Why should he change? He's always denied it before." Bud sighed.

Wright looked more ruffled than usual. "The worst thing about Tovelli is that he claims he's pro-life—you know, personally opposed . . . "

"Yeah, like Pontius Pilate was 'personally opposed' to the crucifixion of Jesus."

"Right. But I think Tovelli is worried about his political skin. He tries so hard to appear impartial in these abortion trials that he goes overboard to protect the pro-aborts. I can get a better deal sometimes from some of the pro-abort judges. I don't like this, Bud. It doesn't look good."

"Pessimist?" Bud asked.

The courtroom door opened, and a gaggle of dark suits entered. In the center, towering above the rest, was Ramsey Briar. With his lean frame, he cut an impressive figure through both the society pages and the courthouse circles. A dark widow's peak split his high forehead. Surrounding him were the president of the state chapter of Family Life and several of the clinic habitués, including Joan Risner and Dr. Piper.

"Jackals!" Bill Wright muttered as he rummaged through the papers in his battered briefcase.

"Hmm?" Bud asked.

"I said, 'Jackals.' Jackals live in desolate places and prey on whatever is weak or already dead. That's what this country is coming to—a haunt of jackals."

"All rise!" the bailiff cried and rattled off the rest of his speech as Judge Peter Tovelli swept in followed by the bulk of his dark robe.

"Be seated," the judge said. "Good morning, Ms. Dunn," he smiled at the assistant district attorney handling the case. Dunn, an attractive, thin blonde with an intense look in her eye, acknowledged the judge's greeting. She always wore unflattering businesslike outfits. Even with glasses, she did not look "bookish," but her legal mind was quick.

Tovelli gravely eyed Bill. "Mr. Wright—well, I suppose that Mr. Wright has a motion or two. You may proceed."

"Your Honor, I move for dismissal based on prejudice. Both the District Attorney, Albert Van Houten, and Ms. Dunn here are known to be actively pro-abortion—"

"Objection, Your Honor. Neither of us are pro-abortion, we are pro-choice—"

"Relax, Ms. Dunn, you cannot object to a motion. You will have ample opportunity to answer to the motion. Proceed, Mr. Wright."

"Certainly, Your Honor. Both are actively pro-abortion. Mr. Van Houten and Dr. Jarvis, the owner of the

Greenbriar clinic where the alleged misconduct took place, are close friends." Bill sat.

"Your Honor," Dunn shrilled, "both Mr. Van Houten and I have supported a woman's right to choose an abortion, but neither of us favors one choice over another. This position leaves us only supporting the law as recognized by the U. S. Supreme Court in *Roe v. Wade*. I fail to see where support of the law disqualifies either of us from executing that law in court."

"Motion denied. You have more I suppose, Mr. Wright."

"Your Honor, I move that a defense of Choice of Evils be allowed according to—"

"I'm aware of the statute, Mr. Wright. Do you intend to present the same evidence as in the past?"

"No, Your Honor, I have substantially more evidence."

"Ms. Dunn?"

"Your Honor, we've been over this ground before with Dr. Tower and his cohorts, several times before you, and it always proves to be a waste of the state's time and money. Abortion is not the issue in this trial. The issues are Trespass and Assault." Janis lowered herself into her seat.

Tovelli momentarily leaned back in his high leather chair, his hair almost matching the black of its upholstery. He straightened. "This is a serious charge against Dr. Tower. In all fairness, I must allow the defense to present evidence as an offer of proof for a Choice of Evils ruling. Are you ready, Mr. Wright?"

"Ready, Your Honor," Bill replied. "First, I'd like to show you a videotaped medical university training film of a second trimester abortion to demonstrate the evil that my client sought to assuage."

"Your Honor, I object to this piece of tape because it

distorts the truth about abortion. Only 8 percent of all abortions are done in the second or third trimester."

Wright retorted, "Your Honor, I have documentation from the state health department showing that fully 24 percent of the abortions performed at Greenbriar are of the kind shown in this film."

"Objection overruled," the judge said wearily, raising his hand. *This is going to be a lo-o-ong trial,* he thought to himself.

The film was gruesome, and the testimony that followed reinforced its message. A fetologist testified that the child is a human being from conception. "There is no possibility that the conceptus would become anything else—a dog, for instance," he said. "This stage of development is simply that—a stage of development. Any first-year fetology student who couldn't tell a human zygote from that of another species would flunk." His testimony on the ability of nine- and ten-week-olds to feel pain made Tovelli cringe inwardly as he thought of the graphic film.

An obstetrician told of his experiences with ultrasound technology, watching the tiny heart beating in the six-week infant, seeing the tiny humans suck their thumbs and react to loud sounds.

The most compelling statements were offered by Darlene Bothwick, who held her sleeping three-week-old child in her arms as she spoke. "If it weren't for Dr. Tower and his friends, I would have killed my baby." She stopped, looked down, and smiled. Then fixing her eyes on the judge, she said, "On top of that, I would be feeling that terrible guilt—again. You see, Your Honor, I've had an abortion before, and I'm only now coming to grips with how badly it had warped my life. With both pregnancies, my situation was about the same—unmarried, no friends, no money. I just didn't know alternatives existed. I didn't hear about them from school or the papers or even Family Life—and especially not at Greenbriar. They mentioned other options as something only a nut would do. Dr. Tower isn't just protesting against abortion; he's saving lives—mothers' *and* babies' lives. My child and I are examples!"

Bill introduced sworn statements from two other women who gave credit to rescue missions for their babies' lives. Objections, arguments, and motions followed one another in long procession as Tovelli, fingers folded tent-like before his face, endured the endless new twists on old arguments. Not that he really had to pay attention. The Choice of Evils defense was clearly out of the question; anarchy, he felt, lay on the side of that decision. Tower would get a fair trial either way, but this little fiction made it look more fair. So when the last evidence was exhibited and the last objection raised, he, the final arbiter of justice in this court, said simply, "Motion denied," and it was all swept away. The jury would never know any of what had been said.

Jury selection finished off the first day.

"I don't think I'll ever get used to that," Bill said, packing his briefcase, "people disqualifying themselves from jury duty because they are pro-life as though that in itself comprised a bias and being pro-abort doesn't. What's worse is that Tovelli already told us that this case has nothing to do with abortion; we can't even bring it up. If that's true, why does being pro-life disqualify a juror? Boy, does the system ever have people snowed."

Bud did not comment. They parted as they left the massive, mock-stone building.

*

The following day, as Bill passed the open door to the judges' chambers, he spied Dunn inside huffing about something to Tovelli. He slid into his place beside Bud, who was already seated at the defense table, and whispered, "Some witches' brew cooking in there." He indicated with his thumb the direction of the judges' chambers. "It's *ex parte*, improper, but what can you do?"

Bud was tense, but it showed only to those who knew him well. The gallery filled slowly. A small cluster formed on the far end of the front two benches—clinic personnel and escorts mostly. And there was Mark Schmalz waving to Bill and Bud as he sat down next to Martha Foreman.

Bill Wright signaled Mark to his side. "Be sure to leave the courtroom as soon as the judge comes in. Witnesses are excluded, and I would hate to have your testimony tossed out. It's really important."

As a pleasant surprise, Pastor John Hite from the Arlington Independent Community Church arrived. Hite's usually serious eyes brightened as he saw Bud. He glided over, took Bud's hand, acknowledged Bill, and said, "I'll be praying."

"Thanks," said Bud noting the wrinkling of the pastor's large forehead, "From what I can see, we'll need it."

"When's the next rescue?" he whispered.

"Next Saturday," Bud replied.

"I'm going."

"Get in touch with Donna Stoner," Bud said. "She'll know what's going on. I could be in jail by then."

The room had filled up. Most were supporters. Some reporters tried to blend into the bare back wall. Bud looked over the group. Then he noticed by the door the small form of Mrs. Roberts. She looked at him piercingly, and the knot in his stomach tightened. He wondered if she were here for the hanging.

The "All rise" rang out.

The judge unceremoniously dismissed the jury into the deliberating room while squinting toward Bud. "Dr. Tower," he asked, "what is that thing on your tie?"

"A tiepin, Your Honor."

"I mean, what is its shape?" Tovelli asked impatiently.

"It's a pair of feet, three-eighths of an inch long, Your Honor. The same size your feet were when you were ten weeks old in the womb. You had a full set of fingerprints—"

"I am going to ask you to remove the symbolic jewelry, Dr. Tower," the judge interrupted, "since this case has nothing to do with abortion. In fact, I will ask that anyone in the courtroom remove any anti-abortion buttons or symbols."

"Your Honor," Bill rose and spoke, "Dr. Tower is wearing a piece of jewelry that you obviously could not see from the bench and that I doubt the jury will be able to see from the box. What purpose does removing it serve? If this trial truly does not concern abortion, why would there be an objection to his wearing a symbol of something that does not concern us here today?"

"It serves my purpose, Mr. Wright," Tovelli said through his teeth. "Those who will not comply will be ejected."

There was some murmuring as those in the gallery removed their pins. Bud made no move. After a moment Tovelli cocked his head and said, "Dr. Tower?"

"Your Honor," he said as he gained his feet, "this pin symbolizes an expression of my religious convictions and is protected speech under two parts of the Bill of Rights of the U. S. Constitution and is protected by our state constitution as well."

"If you refuse to remove it, Dr. Tower," Tovelli said stiffly, "you must remove yourself from my courtroom."

Tower picked up his briefcase, turned, and left.

Once out in the hall, Bud stopped to consider his next move. A small but achingly familiar voice said, "Mr. Tower."

Miss Bergstrom, he thought as he wheeled around. "Mrs. Roberts?" he asked cautiously.

"Mr. Tower," she said, "I just wanted to tell you that some years ago I wasn't so sure about all this anti-abortion work you were involved in, but I prayed about it, and the Lord showed me that you are doing His work. I just want you to know that I've been praying for you ever since. That's why I came today—to pray."

"Well, thank you very much, Mrs. Roberts," Bud said automatically. But inwardly he was surprised, confused, and—more than that—embarrassed. All this time he had misjudged the woman and never once tried to find out if his prejudice had any basis in fact. *Forgive me, Lord,* he prayed inwardly.

"I need to talk with you, to ask your forgiveness about something. I'm headed for another judge's office. Would you walk with me so we can talk?" he asked.

Mrs. Roberts looked puzzled, but said, "Certainly."

*

The opening hours of the prosecution's case was a rote recitation of their witnesses on the trespass charge—establishing who owned the clinic, who had asked Tower to leave, and who had this authority. Standard stuff. Not much for Wright to bite on. The first to even mention the assault charge was Margie Barnes.

"Ms. Barnes," asked Dunn as she stood at her table tapping her palm with a pencil, "do you know Dr. Tower?"

Margie nodded.

"Please answer the question out loud, Ms. Barnes," the judge instructed.

"Yes, I know Dr. Tower," she said.

"How do you know him?"

"Well, he's in front of the clinic with other protesters harassing—"

"Objection, Your Honor," Bill said rising from the leather-backed chair. "There is no evidence that anyone harasses anyone outside the clinic. Dr. Tower has never been charged with or convicted of harassment."

"Objection overruled," Tovelli said wearily. "The witness is obviously just using her own terms, not accusing Dr. Tower of an additional crime. Continue, Ms. Barnes."

"Dr. Tower regularly joins those harassing patients of the clinic. I've also been there twice before when he—Dr. Tower—forced his way in—"

"Objection, Your Honor," Bill rose again. "There is no testimony from Dr. Tower's prior convictions to suggest that he 'forced' entry to the clinic."

"Objection overruled, Mr. Wright. The same reason as before. Should I repeat myself?"

"No, Your Honor." Bill sat.

Dunn walked to the front of her table and leaned back against its edge. She had close-cropped blonde hair, almost what used to be called an ivy-league haircut. Her dark blue suit hung on her body from the shoulder padding, leaving her shapeless. It was hard to imagine her as a woman. She seemed determined to erase every trace of femininity, even in her stiff gait. She removed the oversized horn-rim glasses and said, "Was there anything different about Dr. Tower's actions inside the clinic?"

"Yes," she said, "but I think it is only because—"

"Objection, Your Honor—"

"Sustained. Ms. Barnes, you cannot conjecture on

why things were different, only tell what was different. Continue."

"Well, Dr. Tower always entered the clinic carelessly, but no one ever got in his way before when I was there. This time I was coming from getting a cup of coffee when I saw Joan—Joan Risner—in front of him, and he just pushed her out of the way as he went by. That's when Joan hit her head on the table."

Janis Dunn wrapped up her questioning quickly. The judge broke for lunch. Wright wasted no time locating the indignant Dr. Tower and dragging him to the office of District Court Judge Marvin Columbus.

When court reconvened, the judge lowered himself into his black leather throne. "Dr. Tower, welcome back. Have you removed the pin?"

"Your Honor," Bill interjected, "I have an order from Judge Columbus in this regard. Would you like me to read it?"

"Go ahead," the judge said frowning.

"Skipping the introductions, Your Honor, the text simply says, 'Dr. Tower may wear the pin.'" Brevity was the hallmark of Judge Columbus. Tovelli's face sagged momentarily at the implied rebuke from the higher judge.

"Well, let's get this moving," Tovelli said. "Your cross-examination of Ms. Barnes now, Mr. Wright. Ms. Barnes, you are still under oath."

Bill Wright rose slowly and looked at the easel with its large pad of paper. Running his hand over his balding pate, he walked over and squinted at the black marking on the pad. It represented the ground floor of Greenbriar clinic.

"Ms. Barnes," Bill said, still minutely examining the drawing as though it were a significant document, "you are a volunteer escort at the Greenbriar clinic, is that right?"

"Yes," answered Margie.

"Whom do you escort?"

"Greenbriar's patients," she replied.

"Why do they need to be escorted?" Bill asked turning from the diagram.

"We're there to get the women past the anti-abortion protesters—past their harassment."

"You indicated, in your responses to Ms. Dunn, that Dr. Tower is frequently one of those protesters, am I right?"

"Right."

"Is it your opinion that Dr. Tower and the other protesters are there because they oppose abortion?"

"Yes, it is," Barnes replied.

"Would you say that your reason for volunteer work at Greenbriar is because of your belief in a woman's right to obtain an abortion?"

"Objection, Your Honor," the prosecutor whined. "I fail to see any relevance to this line of questioning. This trial does not concern abortion or abortion protests."

Bill fired back, "Your Honor, it was the state that first broached the subject of the protesters. Since they felt that their presence was connected to this case, I am simply trying to clarify that connection."

"Overruled," Tovelli said with a wave.

"Ms. Barnes, do you remember the question?" Bill asked.

"Yes, I remember. And, yes, I am motivated to be an escort because I believe in abortion as a right—and because I know *they'll* be there," she said pointing in Tower's direction.

Seeing her rising ire, Bill pressed on. "Does that anger you—that 'they'll' be there?"

"Yes."

"Do you think they should be stopped?"

"Yes."

"How badly do you feel they should be stopped?"

"Objection!"

"Sustained. Mr. Wright, you're getting way off the track here."

"Just following the jackal's track," Bill muttered under his breath. "Ms. Barnes," he continued aloud, "you claim that Dr. Tower entered the clinic and walked toward the women in the waiting room and that Ms. Risner got in his way. You further allege that he walked straight on and pushed her down here, is that correct?" Bill's finger was pointing to the place on the diagram where Risner had fallen.

"Well, Joan didn't 'get in his way.' She just happened to be between him and the patients."

"And he just pushed her straight down on her back, right here?" pointing again.

"Right."

"When the doctor came in, did he move her?"

"No," she said. "Well, he straightened her leg, but that was it. He wouldn't let anyone move her."

"How, then, do you explain the fact that Ms. Risner lay—according to the police report—the opposite way from the one in which you describe her?"

"Well, I don't know."

"No more questions, Your Honor," he said.

The next witness was the Mercy Hospital emergency room doctor who had treated Risner that day. His testimony was straightforward—mild concussion, possibility of recurring headaches, and so forth. Wright's only question was equally straightforward: "Doctor, was there anything about the nature of Ms. Risner's injury that would indicate whether its cause was deliberate or accidental?"

"No," the doctor replied as though he had just tasted something bitter.

"The bench will call a recess until tomorrow morning at 9:00 A.M.," Judge Tovelli said after dismissing the doctor. He admonished the jury against discussing the case, got up, and unceremoniously left the courtroom.

"Well, Bud," Bill said over the background bustle of jurors and spectators filing out, "let 'em lie. It's the only weapon they have; we shouldn't begrudge them that. Like the golfers always say, 'Play it where it lies,' eh, Bud?" He watched Bud roll his eyes. "Anyway, we have one eyewitness on your side—Ginger Buck."

"I hate to be the one to tell you," the familiar voice of Grace Wright broke in as she came up to them. "I just got this," she said waving an official-looking paper. "It's an order from the Juvenile Court saying that Ginger cannot testify."

"What?"

"That's right," Grace said. "The counselor the judge ordered for Ginger says that she's psychologically unstable now because of her traumatic problems with the split-up from her mom, the pregnancy, and everything. He took this to the Children's Services, and together they went to the judge, and he signed the order. By the time you get a hearing, Bud's trial will be over. Ginger is heartbroken; she really wanted to help Bud."

Grace frowned as she looked at Bill biting his lower lip and holding his chin between thumb and forefinger. She could see that there would be a long night at the law library for him. He said no more, but walked slowly out.

"Well, why don't you come to our place for dinner, Bud?" Grace said. "I hate eating alone."

＊

A deceptively bright morning sun glared through the courtroom windows the next morning as Bill Wright touched up his shave with a cordless electric razor while viewing himself in the small mirror he carried in his briefcase. It was plenty early, and his small, svelte wife bought his ritual morning coffee from the machine down the hall. An anxious Tower entered the all but empty room.

"Well?"

"Nothing we can do unless Tovelli will help us. Not much chance of that, but worst he can do is say no," Bill explained. "We'll ask."

"Mr. Wright," Judge Tovelli said, "I have no intention of seeing this trial become a Ping-Pong game. We all come under certain disadvantages when other judgments hold sway over our proceedings. If Judge Salizar in Juvenile feels that Ms. Buck is not psychologically up to testifying, we shall all have to abide by her ruling."

Wright could almost feel the knife-twisting delight in Tovelli's rebuke. The judge was obviously still smarting over the rebuff from the District Court over the "little feet" pin.

The state called its last witness, Joan Risner. Wright could see the consternation on her face; she was not settled, as were the other witnesses, on lying about Bud. This offered the glimmer of hope Bill needed. Risner identified Tower from the stand. She seemed to be quoting a script as she described the incident.

"I was just on my way to the porch from the waiting room when Dr. Tower burst in the door. I called for him to stop, but he was already coming toward me. I heard him say, 'Pro-death whore,' just prior to his pushing me down. I went over backwards, and I must have hit the end table, but I don't remember what happened after that until I awoke to see Dr. Piper, the clinic's other doctor, bending over me. All I know is that it hurt, and still does." She rubbed the back of her neck on this last statement, but Wright read the body language of guilt. He suspected that she hadn't felt any pain since a couple of days after the injury. If he could only prove it.

Dr. Piper and the emergency room doctor had already testified about the injuries, but the state depended on written affidavits regarding the extent of the injuries and the current suffering of Joan Risner. These documents were full of cautious qualifiers such as "the patient complains of," "she appears to suffer," and "it is possible that." Wright noted this blatant dodge of legal culpability with humor. *The only suits they want are Italian-made,* he thought.

Bill rose to question Joan. "Ms. Risner, when Dr. Tower allegedly entered the clinic, were you standing about here?" He snapped the pointer on the diagram of the Greenbriar waiting room.

She jumped slightly, startled. "About there, yes."

"Now you say he, the defendant, came from the door, over here, and pushed you backwards, right?"

"Right."

"Would you mind explaining to the court then why the police report has you lying with your head toward the door if you fell back this way?" he asked, striking the pointer again.

Joan faltered, "Well—I don't—well, I'm not sure— maybe the report was wrong?"

"Maybe the report was also wrong about Dr. Tower being there at all, or maybe someone is just lying—"

"Objection," cried the prosecutor as Wright watched Joan quake a little and flush at the last remark.

"Sorry, Your Honor," Bill said with insincere repentance before Tovelli could comment.

"Strike that from the record," the judge ordered, looking askance at the defender.

Bill kept Joan on edge for the rest of the examination, nearly succeeding in dragging the truth from her. He could tell that she almost wanted to tell it. She held out. When Bill had exhausted his questions, Joan seemed exhausted, and the jury probably had questions. Bill could only pray that they were able to see the hesitance that was obvious to him.

With that, the state closed its case, and the defense opened its presentation. Wright had lined up several character witnesses to precede his only remaining witness, Bud Tower. The first, Bud's pastor, had known Tower for eighteen years. The second, a local physician, had grown up with Bud and had referred patients to him. Both gave substantial evidence of the unlikeliness of Tower being violent or behaving in a threatening manner or calling people names. Bill recognized the weakness of this kind of testimony; it appeared egocentric and self-serving. Bill drew out an impressive list of Bud's accomplishments. The jury appeared unmoved.

The judge recessed for the day, leaving the weary Bill Wright the prospect of another long night in search of a legal break. "Things don't look too good for us, Bud."

"Don't take it personally, Bill," Tower said. "The outcome of this trial is in God's hands. If He wants me in jail, there's nothing you can do about it. Maybe He's calling me to a prison ministry."

"True," Bill replied, "but we don't need to go looking for martyrdom."

"Hey, you missed a great beef pie last night at your

house," Bud noted, seeing Bill's morose face. "What do you say I take you to dinner tonight?"

The group left the courthouse chatting amiably, but Bill's mind rarely strayed far from the trial. Finally, he excused himself and headed again for the library.

*

Bud huddled in prayer with supporters before the opening of the third day of the trial. Then the minutes ticked by as they waited for the 9:00 A.M. starting time—that was 10:00 A.M. court time. About 9:50 the bailiff signaled Wright and his nemesis, Dunn, back to the judge's chambers. It seemed that a juror had had car trouble and would be late. Tovelli reset the time for 11:30.

When the court reconvened, the people stood as Judge Tovelli bounded up the steps of the dais. He was spry and slender, his jet black hair belying his fifty-two years. He came in for a landing, quickly spread his papers, and said, "Let's get this show on the road. Mr. Wright, I believe you were about to call a witness?"

"That's right, Your Honor," Bill nodded. "The defense calls Dr. Elgin Tower." A rustle passed through the gallery. The gavel sounded from the bench.

Bud took the oath and was instructed to give his full name, spelling the surname.

"Elgin Grant Tower, T-O-W-E-R," Bud stated flatly.

"Dr. Tower," said Wright, "on the date in question did you enter the building of the Greenbriar abortion clinic?"

"Objection, Your Honor," Dunn said rising to her feet, "the business at 1723 S. Greenbriar is an out-patient surgical center, not an abortion clinic; vasectomies and tubal ligations are also performed there."

"Your Honor, according to Greenbriar's own report-

ing, they do fifteen abortions to one of any other procedure," Bill replied.

"Objection sustained. Counsel will refrain from refer-
ring to the Greenbriar clinic as an abortion clinic," Tovelli
said hardening his expression.

Bill sighed, his strong opening lost on the jury
because of the objection. "Dr. Tower, were you in the
Greenbriar clinic on the date in question?"

"Yes."

"And what," Bill paused significantly, "may I ask, was
your business there?"

"Objection. Counsel is encroaching on the territory
of Choice of Evils."

"Surely, Your Honor, a person's motive is part of his
actions. It was the prosecution that first opened this line
of questioning with Ms. Barnes."

The judge leaned back thoughtfully for a moment,
closing his eyes. Coming forward again, he said, "Mr.
Wright, I will allow no backing into the Choice of Evils
defense. I regard this line of questioning with suspicion.
Your field of inquiry must be very narrow in this area."

"Your Honor, I will endeavor not to *trespass* onto forbidden ground."

"Objection overruled, but be careful, Mr. Wright.
Such a *trespass* would be contempt of court," Tovelli said
returning Bill's pun with seriousness. "Answer the question, Dr. Tower."

Bud followed the exchange with the interest of one
trained in observing human behavior. "I was there because
babies—"

"Objection. The witness is deliberately using the
emotionally charged word, *babies*, to influence the jury
when the accurate term would be *fetus*."

"Sustained," Tovelli said before Wright could utter a

word. "Dr. Tower, once again, abortion is not an issue in this trial. I will not allow inflammatory terminology to color the testimony. You may refer to them as fetuses, if you wish, but not as babies. Answer the question."

Bud responded, "I was there to stop the killing."

"Objection—"

"Dr. Tower," the judge said loosening his collar, the veins in his neck standing out, "the word *killing* is another example of inflammatory language. I forbid it! Just answer the question."

"I went in to stop the slaughter."

"Dr. Tower! I will not speak on this matter again," Tovelli fumed. "I will not be toyed with. You will exclude all inflammatory language—*baby, child, kill, slaughter, murder*—or any like terms. You will also exclude religious argument. There will be no mention of God, Jesus, or any reference at all to deity. I will find you in contempt of court if you continue."

"Your Honor," Bill said, leaning forward on his palms, "my client is just using the terms familiar to him—the same way Ms. Barnes used the word *harass* in earlier testimony."

"The objection *was* sustained, Mr. Wright. Sustained! Need I say more?"

Bud cleared his throat, "Your Honor, no disrespect is intended here, but what can I say?"

"You may say that you were in the clinic because you oppose abortion—that's all!"

"Your Honor, you are putting the words in my client's mouth—this is *his* testimony," Bill said aghast.

"I have simply excluded him from using inflammatory language, Mr. Wright."

"But," Wright stammered, "you've excluded everything that Dr. Tower intends to say. Perhaps you will limit him to the statement, 'I'm guilty'?"

Tovelli reared up, spitting out his words. "I will not quibble with you, Mr. Wright. Nor will I brook any impertinence. The subject is closed."

"I withdraw the question, Your Honor," Bill said resignedly.

The restrictions placed on the wording of each question and answer resulted in over three hours of argument with little significant results. During the final part of the questioning, Bill asked, "Dr. Tower, did you come upon and push Ms. Risner down inside the clinic on the date in question?"

"No," Bud replied. "In fact, Ms. Risner was outside on the porch in her duties as escort. She left the porch to approach a woman who had gotten out of a car about a block away just before I entered the clinic. That was one of the reasons I chose that moment to go in—no one was on the porch. She could only have followed me into the clinic. I was talking to one of Greenbriar's clients at the time. I didn't see how she fell."

"Did she fall," Bill queried, "as the police report said—head toward the door?"

"That was her position when I first saw her, when I checked her pulse, and when Dr. Piper took charge. One of her legs was cocked up underneath her, which Dr. Piper straightened, as Ms. Barnes testified. When I left, she still lay in the same position."

Bill relinquished the questioning to the state's Janis Dunn, who proceeded to badger Bud about his recollection of the incident, then to question his character. "Isn't the violence you displayed just—"

"Objection," Bill cried. "Violence has yet to be proven."

"Overruled. Continue, Ms. Dunn."

"Isn't the violence you displayed just the next logical step in your anti-abortion activities? I mean, first it's picketing, then clinic invasions, civil disobedience, finally, violence—bombs and such?"

"If my only motive were to stop abortions, that might be true," Bud answered calmly. "But I do this out of obedience to God. As distinct from civil disobedience, this is godly obedience. And God has not commanded violence but intervention." Tovelli stiffened at the mention of God, but said nothing.

Bill Wright called his final witness, Mark Schmalz, who clearly testified that he stood directly in front of Greenbriar and watched Risner descend the steps, head toward a car, and turn around cursing after seeing Tower enter the clinic. He had seen her hurriedly reenter the building about thirty seconds behind Tower. The prosecutor was unable to shake his testimony; she turned nasty. "Mr. Schmalz, do you regularly harass the women . . . ?"

"Objection, Your Honor," Bill cried. "Mr. Schmalz has only exercised his rights of free speech and assembly in front of the clinic. He has never been accused of or convicted of harassment."

"Overruled. Continue the question, counselor."

"Do you regularly harass the women entering the clinic by picketing?"

"I picket there—"

"Do you think your testimony here may be influenced by your bias against abortion?" Dunn said with saccharin sweetness.

"I swore to tell the truth—I have done so," Mark answered firmly.

Having planted the proper doubt in the jury's mind, she retreated from the witness lest he display any more of that staunchness of character. She hoped it would be mistaken for stubbornness.

Judge Tovelli appeared relieved. He called for closing arguments; the state went first.

Janis Dunn rose and walked to the jury box, tapping a pencil into the palm of her hand and looking thoughtfully at the stone slab floor. "Ladies and gentlemen of the jury," she said, now looking earnestly into each of their eyes, "as the judge has said, abortion is not the issue in this case—not in the Trespass, not in the Assault. The defendant freely admits that he was illegally on the property, so there is no problem there. But I'm sure you were perceptive enough to see by his testimony the escalating nature of Dr. Tower's anti-abortion fanaticism. And fanaticism it is, since he is no longer able to discern where his rights end and others' begin. It is all very well for Dr. Tower to oppose abortion; it is perfectly acceptable for him to be vocal about it or to educate others about the beliefs he holds. But he began coming to the clinic where troubled women choose to come—greatly agonizing—to terminate a pregnancy because of the difficulties in their lives. And Dr. Tower heaps one last load of guilt on them for their very private choice. But he is not yet content. He later finds he must invade the sanctuary of the clinic for one more chance to impose his threadbare morality on these women. Even this is not enough; he insists on his right to take the law into his own hands by violently and recklessly pushing others around—and finally injuring Ms. Risner.

"You have heard three people, one the victim, testify to these facts. It would be a denial of justice to this whole state if Dr. Tower, who feels it is his God-given right to pick and choose which laws to obey, were acquitted. It would be a grave injustice toward women, who should have the security of privacy in their personal choices. But more than that, it would be demeaning to Joan Risner and all the other women who try to help provide this sanctuary for troubled women if people like Dr. Tower are allowed to destroy that secure place, even violently, with impunity.

"I ask that you find Dr. Tower guilty on both counts."

Dunn retreated and carefully placed herself in her chair. Bill stood abruptly and began speaking on his way out from behind the wooden table. "Well," he said familiarly, "I suppose you understand that it's Ms. Dunn's job to get convictions. Her future could be tied up in how many of them she gets. And I don't envy her either; she has the harder job. She has to show—beyond a reasonable doubt—that the doctor here committed the crime. Unless she can prove that, I don't have to prove anything. And I think she's failed. You probably noticed that according to the police report, the unconscious body of Ms. Risner fell in the opposite direction from what the state's witnesses testified. None of them, including the victim, seemed to be able to explain this reversal. Now police reports are pretty accurate; their whole purpose is accuracy. Both my client and Mr. Schmalz testified that they'd seen Ms. Risner head on down the street, and Mr. Schmalz even saw her go into the clinic after Dr. Tower."

All the time Wright was moving slowly toward the jury. His informality was a powerful part of his ability as a lawyer, but Bill began to doubt its effectiveness as he moved closer to the enclosure and saw the not-quite-hidden hostility in their eyes. "Now you see, ladies and gentlemen," he pushed on, knowing how often he had simply misread faces in the jury or had turned their attitudes around with a quip, "that wily Ms. Dunn over there has tried to get you to think that Mr. Schmalz may have lied because he's pro-life, or somehow that makes him less of a witness, but heck, Ms. Barnes, the Greenbriar escort, is pro-abortion—so that'd make *her* biased too. She even said that something ought to be done about the protesters—the *legal* protesters. That sounds pretty close to infringing on constitutional rights to me. Ms. Risner is pro-abortion as well—and so, for that matter, is the prosecutor herself. She's known to be quite vocal on the subject. What I'm saying is that you can't make assumptions based on whether someone has an opinion. Everyone has opinions.

"But back to the doctor—according to the testimony, it is well known that Dr. Tower is not a violent man. In fact, he is passionately involved in a number of issues and has never done anything violent. He's known to be honest, and he vehemently denies pushing Ms. Risner.

"There is more than reasonable doubt here. There's clear doubt. This man is clearly innocent." Standing now before the box, he half turned, and pointed to the defendant. *If I can at least hang the jury,* he thought, *then maybe I'd be able to get Ginger Buck in on a new trial.*

Bill returned to his chair as the judge's instructions began. "You are only allowed to determine guilt or innocence on the facts of the case; you are not to decide whether the law is right or wrong, whether you agree with the defendant's motives, or let your personal feelings about abortion—"

Bill knew those twisted instructions almost by rote. He knew the judicial system was in serious danger from exactly what was happening right then. Instead of the power of the jury being a check on a rampaging government, it had become a rubber stamp for the judiciary. It had been probably more than a hundred years since people were taught the true function of the jury as both trier of fact *and* trier of law. The jury's power to nullify laws had been, albeit grudgingly, upheld by the U. S. Supreme Court on several occasions, yet the right to tell the jury of this power was withheld jealously by the judges. *What would they do if a jury comes out with the "wrong" verdict?* Bill thought. He knew the government would be powerless to do anything. This was precisely what had happened with the Fugitive Slave Law; it had become unenforceable because juries refused to convict the underground railroad workers who helped slaves escape to free Canada.

Bill expected a longer jury deliberation. In Trespass-only cases it seemed that they only went into the jury room long enough to circle the table and walk out. Assault should take longer. Bill was a little surprised that they were out in only an hour as he watched them file into the box. The foreman handed the chit to the bailiff, and he gave it to the judge. The judge observed a few formalities and turned to face the already standing Bud Tower and Bill Wright. "Dr. Tower, you have been found guilty of Criminal Trespass II, and you have been found guilty of Assault III." Silence held the room.

Then the impersonal tone of the judge cut in, "I'm going to be out of town tomorrow—Friday—so I'll set sentencing for Monday at 9:00 A.M. If you have affairs to clear up over the weekend, Dr. Tower, I hope you are able to post bond of $10,000. I want to assure you are here on Monday."

"Your Honor," Bill began, but Tovelli had already skipped out the door. He turned to Bud. "We'll appeal this atrocity. I'll work on a stay of sentence for the appeal. I'll go the bond—"

"I can handle the bond. Thanks, Bill," Bud said. "What time is it? I've got a counseling appointment tonight."

When the friends in the gallery came to themselves, they huddled around Bud for prayer and then drifted off, shaking their heads.

7 THE BATTLEFIELD OF FLESH

Clarissa's daughter was now eighteen weeks old. Her own rich blood coursed through her veins—type O compared to her mother's A. She would have turned away, hands across her face if light were introduced into her dark, warm home. She was about nine inches long, a small model of the babies people exclaim over, "My, what a darling!" But others would have called her a "blob of tissue," a "product of conception." So her mother thought—her mother, insensate, preparing even now to send her to her doom. The tension raged through her mother's body. A champion—where was a champion to rescue her?

She only felt the tension; she knew nothing of her parents' plans and preparations. Tension was not new. She rubbed her fists into her eyes, smacked her lips, and shrugged herself into a head-down position—for a change.

*

"Mayline, Clare speaking."

"Clare! Your pistol-packin' aunt here. How about lunch—my treat? We'll go to The Gardens. Okay?"

"Sure. But noon hour's busy here, so I can't get away until 1:00 or 1:30."

"No problem. I'll pick you up."

Aunt Jeanne eased up to the curb in her silver-gray Mercedes. It was an older model; she had bought it new before it was the "in" car to have. Clarissa made a short dash through the drizzle to the waiting automobile. She had covered her head with the fashion section of the *News-Clarion*. Almost diving into the seat, she exhaled, closed the door, and said, "Drive on!"

Promptly, Aunt Jeanne floored the accelerator.

"How's the book coming?" Clarissa asked.

"Which one? Oh, you mean the one on gun control and the death penalty," Jeanne answered. "You know, you would think the publishers would be *used* to my cantankerous, opinionated writing—*and* how well it sells—but I'm having trouble getting a publisher again. The other book is going to the printers tomorrow—or so they say. It seems it has been 'going to the printers' for months. You know publishers' time."

"Well, you must imagine that they get nervous, Aunt Jeanne," Clarissa said. "After all, your stands are pretty unconventional on those issues—out in *right* field, you might say."

Jeanne chuckled. "There's nothing 'right field' about freedom, Clare—not about individual or collective freedom to defend yourself."

Jeanne recognized that Clarissa was avoiding talking about herself. "How's it going with Matthew?" she probed.

"I had the laminaria inserted this morning, and Matthew will take me in tomorrow."

"Well, good for you!" Jeanne exclaimed. "But what about how you two are getting along? These kinds of things often run deeper than the issue that brings out the problem."

"Matthew and I talked it over, and he thinks that he just presumed that I would agree with his instant recalculation of our plans," Clarissa answered. "He says he will try not to make assumptions like that again. I think he's wonderful to admit he was wrong."

"For a man, that's unusual," Jeanne answered with a smirk.

Clarissa missed her cynicism. "Well, Matthew is unusual. Still today most men feel the need to run everything, but he wants to really have a partnership. He would no sooner force me *not* to have an abortion than he would force me *to* have one."

"That's the kind of thing women have been fighting for for years. You wouldn't believe how bad things were— even in the sixties," Jeanne added.

"Yeah, I heard that 17,000 women a year were dying from illegal abortions—"

A red Chevrolet cut in front of the Mercedes, and Jeanne sharply but deftly turned the wheel, dodging the offending red blur. "Crazy hot rodders," she muttered. Then she turned back to Clarissa, "So they're saying 17,000 now? Let me give you a little history—unvarnished. Lord knows you won't get it anywhere else. Back when we started the Abortion Rights League in the late sixties, they used to say 5,000. We all knew it was bull, but the press was so enamored with the figure, most couldn't see any reason to correct it. But then one day, a reporter from WDZB called me for an interview, and you know me. I told the truth. You wouldn't believe all the flak I got. I alienated the whole rabid 'wimmin's' wing of the pro-abortion movement."

"You mean—"

"Sure, during the sixties there was rarely more than a hundred a year. You have to go back to the pre-penicillin days to get a figure over a thousand. But all that stuff wasn't the point anyway. Women's freedom to control their own destiny was the point."

Clarissa was quiet for the rest of the drive. Jeanne was aware of the significance of the lull. She added, "Hon, I'm just glad you can have this abortion so freely—and with your husband's support. You two really don't need children right now. You have too many important things to accomplish. You haven't got the time."

The restaurant was no longer busy when they entered its light, airy interior. The hostess in her starched white apron led them to a corner table with a window that looked out on a small garden courtyard filled with vacant tables, anticipating better weather.

Clarissa finally broke the silence. "Why didn't you ever have kids?"

"Well, I usually tell people who ask that nosy question that I hate kids and that 'anyone who loves whiskey and hates dogs and kids can't be all bad'—a quote from W. C. Fields. But, just between us, I couldn't have any. Some people might suspect that it was because of my abortion—it was illegal then—but I don't think so. Anyway, I really like kids but—well, your uncle and I really tried. At first we were too busy—him with his globe-trotting news coverage and me with my 'issues.' When we finally settled down to try to have children, we found we couldn't. The abortion was from before Jack and I got married. It was his, but we had other plans at the time. I guess that's the thing that was difficult for me to accept. I was so sure that the women's movement needed me that I threw away my only chance to have children."

Steering clear of the obvious implications, Clarissa

said, "It must have been awful—having a back-alley abortion."

"Back-alley? Well, it wasn't a coat-hanger version. Most women had their abortions in doctors' offices with up-to-date techniques and equipment. The only thing back-alley about them was that's where the door was that we came and went through. But I think that if we are ever to attain full women's rights just because they are right, we have to stop depending on phony sob stories. I think it's a terrible mistake to scream about going back to coat-hanger abortions. It makes women look hysterical and brainless— that they would go to those methods. They sound stupid— not equal."

Soon they finished their lunch and were once again moving through traffic toward Mayline. The sun had broken through the clouds and was glistening off the wet world.

*

"I got the laminaria in yesterday," Clarissa called from the shower. "There shouldn't be any problems today."

Matthew made an affirmative noise over the hum of his electric razor, wiped off the steamed mirror again, and searched meticulously over his square jaw for any trace of remaining stubble. "Well, don't worry about a thing. I'm going to be there the whole time."

She stepped out of the shower and into a blue terry-cloth robe. Glancing at the clock, she exclaimed, "Oh, we should get going. They want us there about 6:30."

"I still don't understand why it has to be so early," Matthew complained. "Surely, they can't do all the operations at once."

"The woman at the clinic says it's easier to deal with the harassment if everyone comes at the same time," Clarissa explained. "They don't have to have the escorts on duty all day, and once everyone is in, there are fewer problems."

"Wish they would just leave people alone," he commented. "I mean, live and let live. Isn't that in the Bible? Well, I know one thing for sure, they all claim to believe the Bible, but they don't believe when it says 'Judge not.'"

Clarissa thought only of how glad she'd be when all this was over. Her boss, Myrna, had said to her yesterday, "Developing a little tummy there, Clare. Need to do something about that."

She had thought in reply, *You don't know how fast I'll do something about that.* Clarissa actually said, "I will, Myrna." Now she looked out at the soggy day and sighed.

*

The champions for Clarissa's daughter huddled in the dim light of the precipitous gray dawn. They prayed for Life to be victorious—each of them imagining one life, one baby to save.

Bud hardly noticed the patta-patta of the rain on the roof of the van. His considerable shoulders were hunched over as he prayed with the four others who were to block the entrance to Greenbriar that morning. Pastor John Hite, fingers laced together in his lap, prayed, ". . . and we ask that You be glorified today as we do this, Your will, in Jesus' name. Amen."

The chorus added, "Amen."

It was not an inspirational sight, four men and two women huddled in the deteriorating gold and white Dodge van parked in the empty lot of the shopping mall.

The fourth man, Mark Schmalz, was their driver; they would leave their cars here, and Mark would deliver his passengers near the clinic and later collect them at the precinct house. Mark looked worried. "Bud, how's this going to affect your being out on bail?"

"I don't know, Mark, but I do know that this could be my last chance to save a life for a while. The worst they can do is add thirty days to my sentence for another Trespass II after they try me. Either I obey God, or I don't—and I do."

"No reason to sit around here, is there?" Pastor Hite asked. "Crank up this machine and let's go."

The van rumbled to life loudly, clunked into gear, and rolled down the wet, dark street toward the death mill. The few remaining street lights were winking out as the light of dawn crept between the low cloud layers. They had timed their arrival for 6:15, the time when the first woman generally entered the abortionist's lair.

✳

Jennifer didn't know she had a daughter; she just knew she couldn't have anything—son or daughter. Brad had agreed to drop her off in front of Greenbriar. "Call me when you want me to pick you up," he had said. He wasn't being insensitive; he thought that having an abortion was no more serious than having a tooth pulled or tonsils out. That is what "everyone" said. Jennifer had resigned herself to Brad's decision.

Just below consciousness swam the thought, *What would I do if I lost Brad? I don't even have a job.* It was she who could not afford a child right now. Still she felt the quiet tuggings of maternity. As she silently rode toward her daughter's final summons, her empty arms seemed to ache. *If the timing weren't so bad,* Jennifer excused herself. *I'm too young to be chained to a baby. I want those trips to Acapulco. I want Brad.* She looked over at his profile outlined by the glittering, spattered light of the rain-speckled window. A look of deliberate concentration was on his face, deliberate because he sought to avoid serious talk. He was not the modern, sensitive man the media touts, but he was no brute.

The sleek, black Camaro eased its way down the rain-covered streets. Rounding the corner of Greenbriar Street, they could see the bright red brake lights of a van through the oscillating wiper blades. She looked back at Brad, missing the disgorging of five shadowy figures from the van.

*

"No deathscorts," Mark noted as they cruised the front of Greenbriar. "I'll drop you on the next pass."

They circled the block. The gold and white box rolled to a stop before the older home that now housed the clinic. All the windows behind the angry, expanded metal grates were lit. Lacy curtains failed to soften the glare. The oval glass of the front door shone like a beacon, a target. Five dark figures aimed for that spot. They could see several of the staff inside purposefully bustling around. Even had the clinic workers not been so busy, the dim porch light would hardly have warned of the rescue team's presence.

They had arrived before the first escort was positioned on her perch. The plan was to block the door, keeping staff and volunteers inside the clinic, unable to reach the mothers outside. The only other door, a fire exit, was rigged with a crash bar and an alarm. Bud guessed that the clinic manager would never allow a false alarm, even for this cause.

Bud and Pastor Hite stood in the door frame and braced themselves. The three others sat before them. Between Bud's bulk and the pastor's height, the doorway was completely filled. It was only a moment before the staff noted their presence. Though their backs were turned, the rescuers could hear the change in tone of the noises inside the mill. The door swung inward, and the voice of Joan Risner pealed, "Get out of here, Tower. Aren't you in enough trouble already?"

"Joan," Bud replied, "I knew you really believed in what you are doing, but I never thought you would be fanatic enough to lie in court."

Joan reeled. But then she stiffened her resolve. "Some things just cry out to be done," she retorted and slammed the door.

That sound coincided with the noise of a car door opening. Peering out to the street, Bud could see the faint outline of the dark Camaro, its tail lights reflected off the wet pavement. The door stood open and a lone, dark figure emerged. Listening carefully, he could hear, "Call me when you're ready," before the car door struck home. The figure skittered through the rain toward the porch, mounting the steps. Reaching the top, she removed her hat and shook her head, revealing a cascade of auburn hair. Abruptly, she said, "Oh!"

"We're here to help you," Tower began without preamble. "We want you to reconsider killing your baby."

"Hey, I heard about you guys," she said. "Get outta my way!"

"I'm sorry. We can't do that," Bud said shaking his graying head. "We can't just let you go in and make this grave mistake."

"Hey, lissen," she said loudly, "I got a life to get on with. This is my choice."

Once again the door swung wide. Bud felt bodies trying to force an opening between Pastor Hite and him. "We're going to try to get you through here. Just hang on and don't pay attention to these fanatics," said the voice from inside.

"How far along are you?" Bud asked. He reached into his inside coat pocket and drew out a handful of laminated photos. He didn't wait for a reply. "Here's a picture of an eight-week-old baby. Look at the fingers and toes. They can hear this little fellow's heartbeat on instruments at the doctor's office. Is that how old your baby is?" He paused. "Older? How about this ten-week-old? He's got a full set of fingerprints," he said, displaying yet another photo.

Bud noted with relief that the sidewalk counselors had arrived now. "Those people out there can—" He leaned back again against a new assault to break through from the clinic. "Those people can help you overcome the reasons why you feel this abortion is necessary. Is it the money for medical care? We can help. Need a place to go? We can help. You really don't want to kill a little fellow like this. It will haunt you. I know—I'm a counselor, and I have many women who come to me in my practice whose problems stem from abortion. How about this sixteen-week-old baby? Look at that beautiful little girl." He held up the picture just as the head and upper torso of Dr. Piper pushed through between Bud and the pastor.

"Give me your hand," he said. "I'll pull you through. You can just step on these people. They won't hurt you while I'm here."

Jennifer tore her eyes from the picture thinking, *My baby's a week older than that.* She looked at the extended hand of Dr. Piper, then at the picture, then at the hand.

"C'mon, quick," urged the doctor's voice.

Jennifer hung there forever, it seemed. Bud knew that saying more at this critical point would only tip her away from the truth. He just held the picture. She suddenly turned and bolted down the stairs toward the sidewalk counselors. Noting the look on Piper's face, Bud asked, "Lose another few bucks, Doc?" Immediately Bud knew that the remark was wrong. He opened his mouth to apologize.

Piper spat at Bud, drew himself back into the deadly chamber, and slammed the door.

*

Jim Davis had just come on duty and had positioned his prowl car near a troublesome intersection when the call from Greenbriar came over the squawking radio. "Ah-h-h, crap!" he cried aloud. "Not that bunch again." He leaned over, flicked on the light bar, dropped the transmission into drive, and left his spot with flying gravel.

*

The pummeling rain had dwindled, first to a gentle dropping, then to a misty drift, and finally to nothing. Bud watched, satisfied, as Jennifer climbed into the gold and white van with Martha Foreman. Mark brought the beast to life, audible half a block away, and they trundled off to the Crisis Pregnancy Center. In past rescues, the police had arrived almost instantly as though it were a serious emergency. Their zeal had flagged after repetition, and now they began answering these calls according to priority. This, of course, did not please Jarvis, but nothing he could say or do would change that. He simply had to wait his turn.

Bud was the first to see Matthew and Clarissa coming down the street, Matthew's bulk and sweeping arm brushing aside two sidewalk counselors like bowling pins. As they mounted the steps, the pair seemed a little puzzled by the cluster at the door. Then a look of realization passed over their faces simultaneously. But before either could speak, Pastor Hite said, "We're here to help you. We want to save your baby's life—and you a lot of grief."

"Wha—" Matthew began.

Bud looked earnestly at Clarissa. "You really don't need to kill your baby. There are alternatives. We can help. How far along are you?"

Regaining his composure, Matthew growled, "Listen, we don't want to hear this, all right?"

"It's not all right for us to sit idly by while your baby is killed," Bud replied flatly. He turned to Clarissa again and drew a laminated picture from his pocket. "This picture is of a twelve-week-old baby. That's when most abortions happen. This little fellow is no blob of tissue; he has his own fingerprints, brain waves, heartbeat—"

"Gimme that thing." Matthew snatched the photo and tried to rip it in half. Failing that, he flung it off the porch. "You've got no business shoving pictures in my wife's face. I ought to—"

"Maybe you otta, but ya better not, friend," the voice from behind said.

Matthew turned to see the lanky shape of Jim Davis. Both registered shock at seeing the other. "Matt! Say, you folks havin' trouble gettin' in this place? Don't worry, I've handled this bunch before. We'll have you in there in a jiffy."

"Can't you just tell them to leave?" Clarissa asked,

nervously glancing at the picture of the fourteen-week-old baby that Bud now displayed.

"S'pose I could, ma'am," the officer replied, drawing them away from the rescuers, "but I know this bunch, and they'll make us carry 'em away. That there's the famous Dr. Tower—he don' move fer nobody. We'll just have to wait for reinforcements."

Just then the door opened wide again, and the man's voice from within said, "I think we can get the lady through if we work together."

"Wanna try?" Davis asked, cocking his head at the couple.

Both nodded.

Bud and the pastor squeezed themselves into the door frame in preparation for the onslaught. Dr. Piper on the inside forced his arm and shoulder between the bodies of the rescuers. With brief instruction, Matthew joined Davis in pulling the two men outward. Those seated before Bud and the pastor continued to plead with Clarissa as she stood back waiting for an opening. "Please don't kill your baby," they pleaded. One of them held up a picture of the remains of an aborted baby. "This is what's going to happen to your baby," she said.

At length, the gap widened. "Grab my hand," cried Piper. "When I give the word, just step over them."

Two other squad cars and a paddy wagon arrived almost in concert as Clarissa edged between the rescuers' bodies. Matthew could see through the windows as she sat trembling on the chair in the waiting room. He guessed that she was shaken by her ordeal in entering the clinic, but it was the picture of the aborted baby that upset her now. The legend had said "Sixteen Weeks." Her own daughter was eighteen weeks.

The soothing voice of the clinic volunteer broke into

her thoughts. "Relax, everything is okay now." Joan Risner squatted down beside Clarissa, placing one hand on her shoulder and the other on her folded hands. "The police will clean up the garbage outside, and we'll take care of you in here. You look pretty shaken up. Here, just hang on to my hand."

Clarissa nodded.

Outside, the police were officially asking each rescuer to leave before handcuffing and arresting the person. After the three seated figures were removed, Bud and Pastor Hite sat down and went limp. As they cuffed his hands behind his back, Bud noted that the other stalled patients were out on the sidewalk; counselors were doing their work.

Before, when rescuers were carried away, the police picked them up by the armpits. But as Jim Davis wrenched the cuffs down on Bud's wrists, he muttered, "Get ready for a rough ride, Tower." Davis rose, hailed another officer, and grabbing hold of the chain of the handcuffs, said, "Grab him here." They lifted together, driving Tower's face into the porch.

Pain took over Bud's entire body, and he was not even aware of the bellow that he let out. He was dragged face down across the porch and carelessly heaved down the flight of steps to the pavement below. His shoulders were about to dislocate when they arrived at the wagon. Two other officers helped to lift him into the back, exposing the raw scraped face to the the crowd and to the lens of the video camera held by a protester who had managed to tape the entire arrest.

"We've got ya this time, Tower. You've violated your bond conditions," Davis said gleefully, not caring that the camera was rolling. Turning to the cameraman, Davis said, "There's a law against intercepting a communication—it's a felony." He arrested the man and confiscated the equipment.

The man objected, "But I was on a public sidewalk!"

Davis read the man his rights as he handcuffed him and stuffed him in the back of his own squad car.

*

Clarissa's daughter was finally under siege. The war would not be avoided. Her champions had failed.

*

"I guess that the guy showing me what—er—who I was killing kinda turned me around," Jennifer explained as she finished an omelette. "They always told me it was just tissue. I guess I just never really thought about it as a baby."

Martha nodded knowingly. She was gratified to have Jennifer eating as she knew that the girl could not undergo an abortion on a full stomach. Most women didn't return for abortions after having gone this far; they found rescheduling difficult. Sidewalk counselors often took women for a meal on the way to the Crisis Pregnancy Center. It insured that they could not return to Greenbriar, at least that day. The Crossroad Restaurant offered free meals for these women, and the counselors were not shy about using the privilege.

"The story hasn't changed. When I was a nurse at a death mill years ago, I used to double as a counselor. Anybody could be a counselor as long as they could lead the women to have an abortion. 'Does it hurt?' they'd ask. 'No,' I'd lie. 'Is it a baby yet?' they'd ask. 'No,' I'd say. All just variations on those lies. Finally, I couldn't reconcile all that lying to my professed Christianity. The job of putting the baby parts together was bad, but it was the Scripture that called Satan the 'father of lies' that got me. I figured any activity that required lies—so many lies—to keep it going—well, I had to stop.

"With others it's different. I had a friend who had an abortion after her second child—didn't want any more. Her life went straight downhill after that. Severe personality change—started running around—drinking—drugs. Shot her marriage down the tube. She's going to my church now—got back to Jesus. She works with a group called Women Exploited By Abortion that helps women deal with their abortions. If it hadn't been for Christ, she'd be dead—tried suicide twice."

"You used to work in an abortion clinic?" Jennifer asked incredulously.

Martha nodded gravely. Mark, their driver, silently sipped his coffee, leaving Martha to minister.

"So you're doing this to make up for what you did before?"

"Not exactly," Martha replied. "I mean, that is a small part of it, but I first started because I felt responsible as a believer in Christ to offer alternatives to the girls going into those clinics. Jesus offered me an alternative to my former life, so I'm following that example."

"I've never been much on religion, but I suppose if someone is going to be a Christian or whatever, they should be consistent," Jennifer said.

"That's what got me out of the abortion business, Jennifer," Martha said. "I'd become a Christian about two years before I left the business. I have to admit that my church never said much of anything on the subject. The one I go to now says little more. The first church, though, put a lot of pressure on me after I left the clinic and started talking up the subject. They didn't want me to make waves. They said that they felt that the work they were doing in that area was enough. But I never could find out what exactly that work was. There was even a doctor on the board of deacons who did abortions in his office. All this happened about two years after I quit the business. It's hard to find a church willing to get involved at all. Fortunately, I follow Jesus, not churches."

"You keep calling it a business—" Jennifer observed.

Martha, anticipating the rest, said, "It is a business. Five hundred million a year's worth or more. Greenbriar and Family Life both send out paid staff to high schools to promote abortion, but every one of those people's paychecks depends on abortions. In most states, Family Life actually has its own abortion clinics. Big dollars in that business."

Mark cleared his throat meaningfully and drained the last of his coffee.

"Oh! Why don't we get on over to the center and get to work solving those problems of yours, eh?" Martha said, checking her watch.

"Okay."

*

Clarissa looked back at Matthew seated in the waiting room. He was pretending to read a magazine. She'd ducked inside the changing room and slipped into the pale green surgical gown. The assistant arrived quickly and ushered her to the surgery. She'd already signed the three-page consent form without reading it. Now she was being positioned on the table. Dr. Jarvis cruised in, smiled at Clarissa, and opened the chart.

"Hm-m-m," he said, "eighteen weeks. We'll have to go with general anesthetic. Oh, I see you're all set up. We'll start up the anesthetic and get it done." He casually placed the chart on the side table. "This won't take too long. It'll take longer to recover from the anesthetic than to remove the pregnancy. You have someone to drive you home?"

Clarissa nodded.

"Okay," Jarvis said. "We're just going to give you some sodium pentathol intravenously. Then you'll get nitrous oxide. Just relax, this'll be over before you know it."

The pentathol was administered.

Clarissa was beginning to fade out when Jarvis removed the laminaria. He inserted the first in a series of instruments into the cervix to widen it enough to accept the brutal clamp for the abortion.

*

Something was wrong. She felt something touch the bottom of the sac that was her world. Instinctively, she moved away. Then she began feeling a slow artificial drowsiness seeping into her from across the placental barrier. Her mind raced as she fought this creeping heaviness. The sac was pierced, and abruptly, the liquid drained from around her. Her lungs strained to breathe the familiar fluid. Panic seized her mind as her body sought to succumb to the imposed lethargy. A cold metal instrument touched her leg.

*

Dr. Jarvis could see that Clarissa was unconscious. He grasped the pliers-like surgical steel clamp, plunging it into

Clarissa's womb. The looped clamp probed for the infant, and then gripped the umbilical cord. Drawing the instrument out with the cord, Jarvis leaned back until it snapped the cord from Clarissa's daughter, its end spurting blood beyond the catch-basin to the surgery floor. Jarvis tugged the other end loose, dragged it from the baby's sanctuary, and dropped it on the absorbent pad-covered tray. Blood tinted the remaining amniotic fluid pink.

Jarvis drove the instrument back into the womb, feeling, searching. He hummed a snatch of Beethoven. A movement telegraphed itself through the doctor's long pliers to his hand. He clamped onto a tiny leg and crushed down on the thigh, feeling the brutal snap. Jarvis's bicep and forearm tightened as he squeezed down on the instrument.

"Got a limb," he breathed. He twisted his arm side to side several times and gave a jerk. Then he brought forth the appendage with the foot plainly visible. He shook off the piece atop the umbilical cord, where they lay together in bloody sameness. The tool reentered the sanctum and, with a jerk, returned with the grizzly prize—a portion of the chest cavity with backbone and ribs exposed. Another spurt of blood accompanied the removal. Two or three more chunks came, each with a twist and a wrench. Jarvis reinserted the clamp.

"Now for number one," he said using the code for the infant's head. He expertly located the hard ball and crushed the cranium, feeling the crunch through the tongs. As the head was removed, white brain material spilled from the shards of what had been the baby's skull. With the rest of the waste humanity, it was unceremoniously dumped on the tray. Jarvis left the bloody pliers on the instrument tray and picked up the loop-bladed curette. He reached inside the womb, scraping out any remains of

Clarissa's daughter and the evidence of her stay—the placenta. The final parts gushed forth.

"That should be it," Jarvis said snapping off his surgical gloves and tossing them in the waste can. The assistant wiped Clarissa with some gauze pads and dropped them on the tray where the human remains were carelessly heaped. Clarissa was wheeled out. Already, one assistant had pushed the gleaming chrome-plated tray to the side by the sink and began rooting through the crimson heap to insure that the job was complete—that every vestige of the troublesome child had been removed.

Satisfied, she noted it on the chart, folded the absorbent pad over the mangled collage of ripped parts, and casually dropped it atop Jarvis's surgical gloves.

Whistling a tune, the assistant began to clean up the room to make it presentable for the next procedure.

8 FLOTSAM AND JETSAM

From Saturday to Monday, Clarissa's daughter lay—a package of bloody pieces wrapped in bits of gauze, surrounded by the sky-blue backed absorbent pads—encrypted in a metal tomb. The rumble of the engine outside preceded the skre-e-e-crash-bang, shake-rattle-jerk of the dumper lifting the wheeled trash container in the bleak morning light. Even in her burial inside the trash bin, there would be no rest, no peace save the peace of the dead. Her brutally mangled heap of parts, roughly and casually dumped and crushed into the compactor, did not protest.

Bumbling down the street, the truck meandered to the landfill—burial ground of the forgotten. *Are they really forgotten, or does their blood cry to God from the garbage-filled earth?*

∗

Mrs. Roberts knelt beside her bed in prayer for Bud Tower—and the life of the rescue movement. "Have mercy on us, Lord," she pleaded.

*

"Tower!" the guard called into the block-walled holding area. Elgin Tower stood up in his denim pants and plastic sandals, revealing the stenciled PROPERTY OF MARTINA COUNTY on the back of his faded blue shirt. The handcuffs made getting up from the concrete bench difficult. He straightened his shoulders and walked from the harsh fluorescence of the holding room into the moderate glow of the now-familiar paneled courtroom. The guard directed him to the defense table where the rumpled figure of Bill Wright now stood. "I've put in a request for a stay of any jail time pending the outcome of the appeal," he whispered leaning toward Bud's chair. "I couldn't get you out Saturday. Judge said you had violated the terms of your bond. Didn't have much to argue there."

"It's okay," Bud replied. "I didn't expect anything else."

The bailiff entered the room and called, "All rise!" Judge Tovelli seated himself and looked about him at the packed courtroom as the bailiff read the title of the matter at hand. "Well, Dr. Tower, we are about to impose sentence for Assault III and Criminal Trespass II. Your choice of things to do with your weekend on bond was unfortunate. Do you have anything to say before sentence is pronounced?"

"Yes, Your Honor," Bud replied. "I will not plead my innocence of the charges; my innocence before God is assured. But I will address *your* innocence or guilt, Your Honor." Tension crackled throughout the room.

"Since I began rescuing babies a couple of years ago, I have been repeatedly told by well-meaning Christians that I am required by Scripture—Romans 13—to obey the laws of the land. They tell me that government authority is granted by God, and that's true. You couldn't do anything to me if it were not given to you by God. But the same passage that demands obedience of the individual Christian also demands the government's obedience to God.

"Your Honor, you represent that government, and you will stand before the Great Judge and answer for your use or abuse of that power. If you, through government power, protect the wicked, you not only abuse your God-given authority, but you become personally culpable. If you enforce oppressive or unjust laws, you violate the authority of God and undermine your own authority. Beyond that, I have heard you affirm that you are a Christian. This only makes you doubly guilty. I can only say that I am praying for you and your ultimate repentance.

"As for me, I am now, as I have always been, in God's hands. I have obeyed God. I am satisfied with that knowledge and the knowledge that I have helped save human lives. I pray that God will someday grant you such peace, Your Honor."

The room waited in tense silence. Tovelli's stony look revealed none of the doubts that lay within his breast. Someone cleared his throat in the rear of the courtroom; there was a muffled cough and a rustle of cloth.

"Dr. Tower," Tovelli said, ignoring Bud's statement, "you have been found guilty of these two charges. The DA's office recommends that you be sentenced to one year in the penitentiary, three years probation, compensation to the victim, and psychiatric treatment—"

A murmur of horror went through the room. The judge continued, "The State Sentencing Guidelines recommends a maximum of thirty months for a first offense. But, Dr. Tower, you have not only demonstrated a lack of remorse for your misdeeds, but a willingness to add to them in the face of this court's lenience in allowing you bond for the weekend for clearing up your affairs.

"I must confess, it is difficult to decide what to do with intractable persons except to give them prison time. It is with this in mind that I am sentencing you to the full five-year sentence that the law allows—"

The courtroom exploded with sounds. Above them all cracked the gavel until there was order.

"You will also pay restitution to Ms. Risner in the amount of $10,000 and to the Greenbriar clinic in the amount of $5,000. Additionally, you will pay court costs and attorney's fees for Greenbriar. Mr. Wright, your request for a stay of sentence for appeal is denied."

Bud spoke. "Your Honor, I will pay the medical bills of Ms. Risner purely as an act of charity. I admit no fault for her injuries. But not one cent of my money will go to Greenbriar."

"Dr. Tower, until you sign the release for funds, you will not be fully processed by the penitentiary. You will be treated as a noncooperative and kept in solitary confinement," the judge warned.

"So be it."

*

Bud's supporters clustered in knots around the court-room. Pastor John Hite snagged several of the most active pro-lifers on a pass through the crowd. "Meet me over there," he pointed. When they all arrived, he said, "We can't let this sentence slow us down. If anything, we have to come on stronger. More rescues. I intend to be as troublesome to this bloodthirsty system as Bud was."

"I'm with you," Mark Schmalz added quietly. "How about a rescue this Saturday? We'll be double trouble."

Others chimed in, and soon it appeared that next Saturday a record twenty people would stop abortions at Greenbriar.

*

Joan Risner thought of the day's events—the necessity of it all. Since she had been on the stand, she had not felt any twinges of guilt for her "creative testimony." In fact, she was beginning to share the same sense of "high calling" to a noble cause that everyone else seemed to feel, though, for reasons she could not explain, she left early from the boisterous, smoke-filled victory party in favor of the solitude of her own home.

She felt washed out. "Yes," she had assured the anxious inquirers as she left, "I'm fine—just very tired. It will feel good to curl up with a book and Bach in my own living room."

Joan *was* tired. She leaned back against the cushions in her darkened living room and punched the "play" button on the stereo. Soon the contrast of the severe and subtle beginnings of Bach's *Toccata* and *Fugue in D Minor* began to strain from the speakers. *What an incredible piece,* she thought. A glow of satisfaction came over her as she remembered Tower's sentence.

But as the music grew in intensity, so did disruptive thoughts. The eerie multiple violin strains of the music reminded her of the conspiratorial air of a movie, *Rollerball,* she had seen years ago. She, too, was part of a conspiracy. But the movie had shown that even the grandest plot could backfire. In the movie, the evil cabal had tried to rid themselves of Jonathan, a singular sports champion, and what he stood for, but their very scheme had resulted in Jonathan's greater victory.

The book dropped from her hand, and Joan fell asleep with the music and these very disturbing thoughts. She awoke suddenly. *Was that a baby crying?*

*

Dr. Jerry Piper wadded up the resignation he had typed for Greenbriar Surgicenter and tossed it in the wastebasket—just as he had done a dozen or so times before.

*

Jennifer sat back in the overstuffed chair, sipping the steamy hot herb tea from a cup that rested between sips on the small roundness of her belly. She paid scant attention to the blather of the evening news as she snuggled down in the wood-stove warmth of the family room. She heard the door close behind Dennis Martin as he left for his shift at the taxi garage. The Martin family who had taken her in was already immense, seven kids, but they seemed to all rejoice in the stretch to include one more. Brad's predictable response had not left her homeless. Martha had told her that there were many families who wanted to help girls in her position. The Center was working on getting her some job training. A doctor was already lined up.

Her future was not looking as bleak as it had when she stepped onto Greenbriar's porch thinking she had no choice but an abortion. She had attended church yesterday with the Martins. It wasn't boring at all.

Out of the corner of her eye, she saw the face of Bud Tower on the television. She leaned forward to hear the newscaster say, "Judge Tovelli, in an unusual move today, gave the maximum sentence of five years to the first-time assault offender, Dr. Elgin Tower. The judge remarked on Tower's lack of remorse as key to his decision. Defense Attorney Bill Wright says that Tower is glad to have been able to help, in his words, to 'save human lives.' The victim of Tower's assault, Joan Risner, refused comment, but pro-choice leaders called it a victory against clinic violence."

Jennifer sat back contemplating the news. Just then she felt the rolling kick of her daughter against her abdomen. She knew then that she would raise her own child, and she would raise her pro-life.

*

That very night, as Clarissa slept, she dreamed.

She knew she was in the waiting room of the Greenbriar clinic, the potted ferns hanging perfectly from the ceiling, brass lamps gleaming on the corner and end tables. The room was filled with spectators, rows of them on bleachers. The atmosphere was a cloudy amniotic fluid—she knew without being told. The watchers on the bleachers gasped in unison as a burst of blood escaped from the surgery into the waiting room. Clarissa watched herself rise and move as through molasses toward the room. She felt her panic as she cried, "You don't understand. It had to be done!"

When she reached the point halfway across the room, the surgery door swung open, and out drifted a leg, an arm, a crushed head, another arm, each going its separate way. Desperately, Clarissa tried to capture and conceal each piece while the crowd screamed, "Was convenience worth *this?*" At last she found the head. As she approached, its crushed appearance changed, reformed to the perfect baby face. Suddenly, her own face was inches from the infant's closed eyes. The eyes opened, the mouth opened, and she cried.

Clarissa awoke.

AFTERWORD

This story is not really fiction. I have merely compiled true stories from within the pro-life movement. The characters and places themselves are fictional, but the events have happened—in large part—as I have described. A young pregnant mother *did* fight the system and her mother for the right *not* to have an abortion. She won because of *Roe v. Wade!* I have spoken with individuals and counselors who have described the dreams of Postabortion Syndrome women. Judges *have* ordered pro-lifers to remove all pro-life and religious symbols while in court. Sentences of five years for rescues have been handed down. Peaceful rescuers have been falsely accused of assault. And, most important of all, babies are real people from conception on.

All I have done is to weave the true stories I know into this tale. Much more bizarre things have happened since I finished the book, and some of what happens here to pro-lifers seems tame by comparison. One fact, however, has not changed—babies are literally ripped apart daily. Until they get justice, how can any of us hope for it?

Paul deParrie
Portland, Oregon
July 27, 1990